Jonah's Bride

JILLIAN HART

Copyright © 2011 By Jillian Hart

First Published 1999
By Zebra Books Kensington Publishing Corp.

Cover art by Kimberly Killion, Hot Damn Designs

Book formatted by Jessica Lewis
http://www.Author'sLifeSaver.com

All rights reserved.

ISBN-13: 978-1490346472
ISBN-10: 1490346473

CHAPTER ONE

Movement caught his eye. A trickle of leaves. A sway of a bough in the nighttime forest. Jonah Hunter gripped his musket by the wooden stock, his senses alert. Perhaps it was his years serving in the militia, fighting Indians, fighting the French, that made his blood turn to ice and awareness prickle down the back of his neck even here in these peaceful Connecticut woods. He was battle weary, and yet the soldier within him still lived.

Danger. He sensed it as surely as a wolf scenting prey. Snow shifted through the reaching limbs overhead, blotting out the half moon's light. A chill raced through him. He stepped forward, following instinct and the soft, barely audible pad of footsteps.

"State your business, man." Jonah braced his feet, musket already loaded, his hand steady.

No answer. No sound other than the wind through the trees and the snow tapping to the frozen ground. This was Puritan land, bound by a nine o'clock curfew. No decent man would have midnight business to conduct on these roads—but he did.

Jonah Hunter was no decent man.

"I have little patience. Show your face, coward."

Still no answer.

The wind stilled. The night silenced. Tiny hairs on his forearms and the back of his neck stood. Something felt wrong. Deadly wrong. And it wasn't the soft pad of timid footsteps trailing through the forest, one step at a time away from him. Jonah hefted his musket and followed the coward's path.

A damned clever coward, winding through the trees with hardly a sound and a lightness of step. It was the whisper of fabric that took him a moment to place—then he recognized the rustle of a woman's skirt. He could feel her presence like the shadows of the trees crowding him. Not so far away she stood, there by the old alder, fear drawing her breath shallow.

"What foul business are you about tonight, mistress?" he asked, highly amused he was chasing nothing more than a woman through the forest.

A twig cracked. Her footsteps stormed nearer. She rose like a shadow from the ink-black night. "Jonah Hunter. I recognize your voice, you scoundrel in a gentleman's cloak."

He chuckled and lowered his musket. Lord, had it been a lifetime since he last laughed? Jonah shook his head and stepped back lest she stormed right over him. "Tessa Bradford. Only you would be so bold as to call me scoundrel."

" 'Tis only the truth." She stormed to a stop before him, chin high, yet her voice wobbled when she spoke. There was no hiding some fear. "I am quite capable of spotting a devil when I see one."

"A devil?" Intrigued now, Jonah reached out and snared the angled shadow of her elbow. Beneath woolen cloak damp with snow, he felt the flesh and bone of a woman. Solid. Intoxicating.

Hell's hounds! If he thought this female attractive, he'd been traveling too bloody long without food. Hunger was sure to be affecting his reasoning.

"Jonah, get your hands off me." She fought, trying to twist her arm from his grip with a surprising amount of strength. "I will not have you compromising my reputation."

"Yes, after all, we must protect your pristine reputation." He tightened his hold. He would not release her. Danger still pricked his spine. The night was as silent as death and that worried him. "Tell me, what is such a proper woman doing alone and unescorted at this time of night? Up to mischief, no doubt, and I—"

Something hard struck him above his left temple. That hard something splintered, and he recognized the scent of rotting wood as pain ricocheted through his skull. She'd hit him. And damned hard. Jonah's knees wobbled. His grip eased. And she fled, crackling through the forest with the speed of a bird.

What the devil was the woman about? He'd been gone from this backwoods village for over ten years—hadn't thought of her for more years than that and wouldn't have wanted to. Now, his first night back to the township he called home, he had to endure—

A swish of a shadow caught his eye, hugging the ground, moving fast and low, trailing after her.

Tessa Bradford, the most sharp-tongued, stubborn woman in all of Connecticut Colony could rain down more trouble on a man than she was worth. Jonah snatched up his musket and bounded after her, reaching for his horn of gunpowder, cursing her with each step.

Harebrained. Infuriating. Troublemaking.

He fell to his knees, straining to see through the sting of heavily falling snow. The woods had given way to meadowland—and he easily spotted Tessa's dark figure silhouetted against the snow-laden ground. Without doubt, he aimed his musket and squeezed. A flash of fire, a roar of thunder, and the wooden stock kicked hard into his shoulder.

In the deafening silence, the snow clouds overhead broke apart, unveiling the half moon. Light washed across her back as she turned to face him. Her mouth opened, her mittened hands balled into outraged fists.

That was a gunshot. Tessa's gaze froze on the sight of broad-shouldered Jonah Hunter kneeling in the snow, reloading his musket.

Panic froze her up like an icicle. The man was daft. Much worse now than he was before he left the village. What sort of man shot at a woman? Surely he didn't—

Across the meadow Jonah Hunter lifted his musket and aimed it. Directly at her. For the second time.

"Jonah!" She opened her mouth, but her throat tightened. She could not scream, could only whisper as the eye of his musket found her. Sensation crawled across her skull. Time froze as she felt the shadow rise up behind her. Fire and thunder flashed through the night and a heavy weight struck her between the shoulders. Air rattled from her lungs. Pain slammed down her spine. She fell face first into the snow, driven there by the dead weight on her back.

Big black boots thudded closer. Tessa concentrated on Jonah's approach, her chest convulsing, tears rolling down her face. She couldn't breathe. Air knotted in her throat. She could not draw it deeper. She coughed and sputtered, certain she'd drawn her last breath. *Had this madman shot her?* Pain cracked like thunder through her chest and up her windpipe with each coughing gasp.

Tessa lashed out when his big hand touched her forehead. She didn't want his help. Not now. Not ever. God, she was going to die, an unremorseful spinster, right here at the feet of wicked Jonah Hunter, without family or friends who would mourn her. Somehow a sob wedged itself in her broken chest. How could he do this to her? How could he—

The weight lifted from her back. Tessa raised her chin from the snow and eyed the dark shape lifeless on the earth beside her.

"Be grateful I am a damn good shot, Tessa Bradford," Jonah's rumbling voice filled the silence of the night. "Or you would be supper for a pack of hungry wolves. And what a poor supper you would make, you are such a tough, skinny little thing."

Oh, she would set him straight with a few choice words if she could catch her breath. Eyeing the dead wolf, her panic eased. He hadn't shot her after all. He hadn't—

Relief slipped through her, cold and sustaining. The spasm in her chest eased some. She felt the damp night cold penetrate her woolen cloak, and the smell of winter earth filled her nostrils. Thankfully, she drew a single shaky breath.

"Of all the damn fool things to do," she sputtered, hoisting herself up on both elbows. "You could have missed and shot me instead."

" 'Tis a comfort to know you can use your tongue as a weapon even with the wind knocked out of you." Jonah's big fingers curled around her upper arm.

Tessa tilted her head back. Filtered moonlight silvered the black length of his hair and shadowed his strong-planed face. Oh, how he'd changed over the years. Grown wider of shoulder and girth, become more handsome. It was his eyes she remembered, brown like the earth and more elemental.

"Slowly, now," he said, almost kindly, as he helped her to her feet.

Jonah Hunter kind? As if the devil could change sides.

"I needn't your advice," she said quietly. It would be so easy to lash out at him, but her gaze landed on the lifeless animal's body. "You shot twice."

"And killed two wolves." His hand lighted on her shoulder.

Heat seared through layers of wool and flannel to scorch her skin beneath. Tessa managed a shallow breath. "Two wolves?"

"Seems you attracted the attention of the entire pack." Low, powerful, Jonah's voice sailed. He studied the ground behind them. "See? The wolves have already claimed the first body. There are tracks."

Tessa was not interested, but her gaze slid downward, past the width of Jonah's chest to the snow-covered earth. A maze of prints covered her own in the moonlit snow. Maybe a dozen creatures, she guessed. Made bold by hunger.

Icy fear shivered over her skin. "They would have—" She couldn't finish the sentence. Her knees began to wobble. Her eyes teared. Death had been so close. The wolf—the one that had landed on her back—it must have been pouncing when Jonah's bullet snatched it out of the air. She would be dead, gone without a trace or a proper burial, if not for Jonah Hunter.

"You are safe now." His second hand landed on her shoulder and he drew her against him.

Locked in his arms, her cheek pressed against his snow-damp cloak and the solid chest beneath. Tessa closed her eyes. Silly to let him hold her this way. Silly to think she needed any comfort. But her fists filled with his cloak and she could not force herself to step away.

"You saved my life," she whispered. "I—"

"Jonah!" A faraway voice split the night's air.

Only after Tessa stepped away from his solid chest and out of his comforting embrace did she hear the drum of footsteps on the frozen earth. Her senses spinning, panic rising, she took another step back toward the heavy shadows.

The boys who'd been skating on the frozen pond at the far end of the meadow heard the shots and were coming to investigate.

Boys from the village. Would they recognize her even in the dark? Would they talk? And would that talk get back to her grandfather and every one of the selectmen of the village? Fear quickened the beat of her heart. Oh, why had she been so foolish? Even to escape the prison of her grandfather's home?

Jonah shielded her with his big body, casting her more deeply in shadow. The din of the approaching boys shattered the forest's peace and frightened her more.

"Go," he said. "Before you land yourself in more trouble."

Her heart twisted. So, he understood. To be caught with him alone in these woods would mean nothing short of disaster. "Th-thank you."

Even in the dark, the light in Jonah's eyes gleamed. "Remember this. You owe me, Tessa Bradford. There is no good deed done without a price."

A chill snaked down Tessa's spine. His words frightened her. He frightened her. What did he mean? What price would he expect for saving her life? Feeling as if she'd just bargained with the devil, Tessa slipped into the shadows and escaped just as the boys gathered around Jonah, already spinning tales of heroism.

CHAPTER TWO

Jonah stepped foot in the pitch-black room, apprehension a tight ball in his chest. He'd been too long from this house in which he'd grown from boy to man, too long disappointing the one man he loved above all. "Father?"

"I am here, boy."

Jonah's conscience twisted at the raspy sound of his once strong papa's voice. He stepped carefully, moving by feel rather than memory through the parlor. Strange to think he'd come home for good.

"I have been awaiting your return." Father's breath drew short and shallow, filling the dark room.

I have failed him. The knowledge defeated what still lived in his heart. Jonah's throat filled. *I should have come home. I should have made Fathers life easier.* And yet being a soldier, that's what Father had wanted for his firstborn son.

"I would have been home sooner." Jonah fisted his hands. "There were . . . complications."

"Always are in war."

"I was wounded," he confessed. But held back the truth that would shame his father, that he had not liked soldiering.

"As long as you have all your parts, son." Father's chuckle came like a cough, but humor still sparkled in his voice "I can think of only one appendage a man cannot live without."

" 'Tis true." Jonah saw nothing humorous about his father's health, about the sadness filling the room like smoke. "I have come to care for you, Papa."

" 'Tis high time too, boy." Withered hands, once so powerful, gripped his—hard and needy, the way a child might. "I have missed you, Jonah."

"That is why I've come home." He felt both the aching loneliness and the weakness in his father's grip. All these years while he'd been gone proving himself, his father had turned into an old sick man.

I never should have left him. I never should have—

"Now that you are here, will you stay, boy?"

"I intend to be the son you need, as always." Jonah felt resolve ball in his chest, tight and sustaining. Promises. They did not come easy to him, but when he gave his word, he would die before breaking it. "Tell me what you want, Father, and I will do it."

A cough rent the air, filling Jonah's heart with dread. The frail man sputtered for breath, then settled back in his chair, exhausted. The moonlight slipping through the diamond shaped windowpanes illuminated the weary circles beneath his half-closed eyes.

When he spoke, his voice was a scarce whisper. "This land is everything, Jonah. My father claimed this piece of earth not by handing over money in exchange for it, nay, he paid for it with his life, with the strength in his back, clearing this wilderness with naught more than an ax. He braved starvation and illness and wild animals. He earned this land with every drop of his blood and sweat shed for it. I have fought my battles for this land, too."

"Father, I—"

"Jonah, I raised you to be independent, an American, to think for yourself. When you, as a grown man, asked to leave, I let you go. For ten long years you have made your way in the world and I asked nothing of you until now."

Admiration for his father burned in his chest. Jonah's throat closed, and he tightened his grip on the old man's hands. He loved his father, who had loved him all his life no matter the mistakes he made, who always forgave him. A son—a man—could not ask for more.

"Find yourself a wife, Jonah, bring her here before I die. Fill this house with children. Promise me. You are my first son, Jonah. This land is your inheritance, and family is your duty."

Father fell silent, yet the moonlight did not hide the gleam of tears on his cheeks.

Jonah settled heavily to his knees. The words balled in his throat, words he'd meant to tell his father. Of the killing a soldier had to do. Of his life. Of why he could truly never call any place home again.

But duty—and the sadness on his father's face—kept him silent about his past.

"I vow it, Father. I will take a wife."

* * *

Her cloak was ruined. There was no saving it. The thick stain of blood from the wolf had soaked into the weave of the fabric. No amount of her homemade lye soap would remove it, even though she'd been scrubbing for two long hours.

Tessa hung her head, defeated. Dawn would come and with it a new day. How would she explain the ruined garment? She had no other. Surely Grandfather would notice her lack of a cloak during this morning's frigid walk to Sunday meeting.

She stood and hung the ruined length of wool to dry in the cow's stall. No one in the family would notice it there. With a heavy heart, she lifted the bucket of lye water.

Did she regret last night? She was foolish for her adventure, but she'd only wanted a brief escape from her grandfather's unhappy home. To skate on the ice and be free, just for a spell. Then the boys came and she had been scurrying off when Jonah Hunter found her.

Jonah Hunter. He was a handsome one. And what a foolish thought! She was too old for romance. No one, especially one so fine, would marry her. She was lucky to live under her stern grandfather's roof, even if she still wished . . . oh, how she wished, for what could never be.

But what if Jonah Hunter spoke of her midnight adventure? Tessa's meager hopes sank. If he did and Grandfather learned of what she'd done, then there would be no more midnight adventures, no swirling alone on the ice beneath the stars.

The cow shifted in her stall. The horse kicked, hoof against wood. Something was wrong. It was too early for Grandfather to be up for his chores. A scraping sound rasped along the edge of the stable.

Another hungry wolf? Mayhap a bear? She gripped her pail

more tightly and hurried toward the unbolted door. The rasping sound ceased. Tessa froze, listening. Mayhap whatever it was had vanished, been frightened by the sound of her approach.

A groan of wood. A whisper of the leather hinges. *Something was opening the door.* In the flickering lantern light she could see a tall shadow, a big hand nudging the door wider.

"Grandfather?" she whispered.

"Not in your wildest dreams." Jonah Hunter strode into the stable, dressed in a large black coat that fell to the top of his fine leather boots.

"*You.*" Her step faltered. "You have no right to step foot near me, Jonah Hunter."

"After saving your life, I have every right. You owe me, Tessa Bradford. And I require payment. *Now.*"

"Payment?" Fear fluttered in her chest. What did he want?

"Yes, payment." He stalked closer, all darkness and might.

"Now? I have no money."

"I do not require money." Still he approached.

She shrank into the shadows. He didn't want any money? "Then what do you want?"

"You, Tessa Bradford." His voice shivered over her like candlelight, brief but caressing. "I want you."

Heavens, he wanted her virginity. Tessa froze. Air caught in her chest. She couldn't breathe, she couldn't speak. Did he think he could just walk in here and demand her virtue?

"Where is your cloak?"

He towered over her, enormous in the shadows. Tongues of weak light caressed half his face. Standing partly in the light and shadowed by the dark, he seemed more beast than man.

Tessa's hand flew to her throat. Every instinct clenched tight in her gut. It was sensible to be afraid. Rumors of Jonah's imminent return to Baybrooke had grown to legends. Major Hunter, who had killed Indians, saved mothers and helpless babes from scalping, fought bravely for the Crown and the colonies.

No man with eyes so dark could be trusted.

"My cloak is wet." Her throat choked out the words, "R-ruined. F-from the wolf."

Jonah shrugged off his cloak and swung the fine length of cloth around her shoulders. "Here, this will keep you warm. The night is cold and we have a far way to go."

"Go? But I have my chores here." Tessa lifted her chin.

"Then they will wait until you return." His fingers curled around the back of her neck, hot and possessive.

The thought of touching him made panic squeeze tight in her chest She dropped her bucket, the lye water spilling into the straw at her feet. She swallowed, time slowing as her gaze focused on the wide column of his neck. A strong pulse beat beneath his dark skin. Jonah Hunter was a vital man, with a man's appetites.

"Please." Fear beat at her heart.

The strength of his fingers cupped the base of her skull and nudged her head back. Her gaze collided with his.

"I need you tonight, Tessa." A flicker of light hopped across his face, and she saw a steadiness in his bold eyes. A trueness that made the uncertainty drain from her chest.

" 'Tis not right for me to be out in the night with you, Jonah Hunter," she argued quietly. "Regardless of what you need."

In the webby darkness, his face changed. "Then we'll make a bargain tonight. A pact between you and me."

Outrageous. "Only the devil makes bargains."

"Is that what you think I am?" His laughter knelled deep and rich as rum. Amusement glittered in his eyes and he did not seem so dangerous. He seemed . . . human.

Tessa relaxed, felt the heat of his fingers biting into the back of her neck, smelled the horse and night scent of him.

"Trust me. I am nothing more than a flawed man."

She considered that. Considered him standing before her as brash as the night. "A very flawed man."

"Deeply so." Jonah's hand settled on her shoulder. Solid. Unyielding. "Will you come?"

The heat of his skin burned through the thin layers of wool and flannel. She would be dead if not for his steady aim. Tessa closed her eyes. Her heart stopped at the memory of him kneeling in the moonlight looking as solid as a legendary hero, musket aimed and then firing.

He'd saved her life with those two shots. Still, Tessa was not like her mother. "I will not go with you. I will not trade my innocence for my life."

"Innocence?" Jonah shook his head, scattering his long black locks over the stunning breadth of his shoulders. Then merry laughter filled the air. "Let me understand this. You think I want to bed you?"

" 'Tis no laughing matter." Tessa curled her fists, ready to fight for her honor. "I will never give you that. My innocence belongs to the man who will be my husband one day."

He only laughed harder.

What was so funny? What could possibly be—

Then she knew. Jonah Hunter hadn't wanted her maidenhood. The very thought made him howl with laughter. Why, he must think her ugly, like every other man in this horrible village. Shame jammed against her heart and she spun away, walking fast, blinking hard.

"Tessa." She heard his step, felt the thud of the earth as he approached.

She kept walking. Pain wedged in her throat. Who did he think he was? He might be one of the richest men this side of Boston but did that give him the right to hurt her feelings? Make her think a man so fine would want her?

Well, she wasn't worthless. What she lacked in looks, she made up in heart, in loyalty. She was too good for the likes of him, fine cloak or no.

Anger bubbled in her chest. "I am no longer a schoolgirl, Hunter, and you have no right to hurt my feelings just as you did years ago when you were a wretchedly behaved schoolboy."

"Tessa, I know. I'm sorry." Jonah choked down his last amused chuckle. His voice came light, not teasing, but not serious either. "You are right. I was a wretched little boy."

"And a wretched man." She paused at the well, curling both hands around the handle. Aye, she might be skinny and disagreeable and probably ugly, but she still had feelings. No man—no matter how fine the cut of his jacket—seemed able to understand that.

A big hand covered hers. Male-hot. Possessive.

"I am truly sorry, Tessa." Sincerity lined his hard cut face, at odds with the devil's light in his eyes. "I did not mean to hurt you. I only meant—" He sighed. "I require other services from you tonight Grab your herbs or whatever concoctions you use. My father is ill."

Anger drained from her chest. So, he didn't want her intimately. There was no surprise in that. The old pain of not being wanted clutched at her heart. She knew that pain would show in her eyes, and she thanked the night for hiding it from Jonah's sharp gaze. How could she have been so foolish? There wasn't one man alive who'd ever shown a romantic, even a practical interest in her.

Jonah caught the collar of his cloak and rested it on her shoulders. He stood so tall, felt so big.

"Tessa. Will you help me?"

"Yes." She would help anyone who was ill. How could she do less? "But Grandfather will not permit me to go until morning."

"Damn Ely. You are coming with me now."

"Jonah, we both know I cannot. 'Tis not proper. People will think—"

"I don't give a damn what people think. Come with me now, and I vow to remain quiet about finding you in the forest tonight. That is our deal, our pact. Decide now, or I will wake your grandfather."

Oh, she hated him. She truly did. Beneath the layers of tailored wool and finely woven cloth Jonah was no better of a man than her grandfather, than others who'd had power over her and used it. "Let me get my basket."

She stormed away, fists curled in anger. Life would be different if she'd been able to marry, if she'd been free to be courted like the other girls. All her school friends were married and mothers of children.

Foolish to feel sorry for herself. She'd not been free to marry, not with Mother so ill. No amount of sadness could change the past. Tessa snatched her basket of herbs from her own corner of the stable.

Jonah Hunter rose above her, dark as the night, mounted high on his fine stepping horse. Even in the shadows, the animal's coat shone.

"Hand me your basket," he called.

She lifted it. Their fingers met. Dazzling heat popped along her skin at his touch. Such foolishness, she scolded herself. Jonah Hunter had laughed at her. He would never care for a woman so plain.

"Hurry. My father's illness cannot wait." He set the basket on his firmly muscled thigh.

And what a thigh it was. Tessa blushed, shocked at herself for noticing.

"Am I to walk?" she demanded.

"No." A naughty grin tugged at his beautiful mouth. "You shall ride on the horse . . . behind me."

A mistake. Even an hour later with dawn's light pink in the east, Jonah could still feel the entire length of his back tingle where Tessa had leaned shyly against him during the long ride home.

True, she'd refused such a proposition at first, but when he would not dismount and offer her the horse and after a quarter mile walk, she'd relented. Even now, his blood felt thick from the way her slim body had rocked against his, so soft and feminine.

Hell, he'd had enough women to know none of them should affect a man so. What the hell was wrong with him? Jonah rubbed his hands over his face, exhausted, half sick with hunger and worry. Too much on his mind, too many responsibilities, and too much guilt. He thought of the frail, sick man upstairs and his chest squeezed tight. Why hadn't one of his errant brothers written of Father's condition?

What the hell was taking so long? He'd been twice to his father's cold bedchamber to see Tessa sitting at the old man's side, an oddly comforting presence.

Tessa Bradford had stood for no nonsense back in dame school when he'd pulled her braids, and to no one's surprise she'd grown up into a woman no different.

Yet he'd stood in the hallway, entranced by the lure in her soothing voice. Why, 'twas a different woman. Gentle lamplight had made her stern face kind, brushing at the softness of her cheeks and the shape of her Cupid's-bow mouth. Jet-black curls fell untamed from her cap, shimmering in the flickering light. Only angels looked so unabashedly unselfish. How could this unearthly creature be Tessa Bradford?

She bent to her work, unaware of his presence in the shadowy hallway. Worry pinched her soft face as she smeared a pungent paste of some sort on Father's bare chest. A tart, unpleasant smell filled the room, hurting his nostrils. But Hell's teeth, he could not tear his gaze from the sight of her.

How long had it been since he'd witnessed such gentleness? Jonah's eyes teared at the memory. It had been his mother, the gentle woman she'd been before illness claimed her. He'd been a mere boy, but he remembered the love in her hands whenever she would brush the curls from his eyes. Whenever she baked tarts small and tasty for a little boy's sweet tooth.

The old man stirred, and Tessa Bradford brushed a gentle hand over Father's forehead. Such a caring gesture that it made Jonah's heart rend. Aye, the old man was desperately ill. They all knew it.

"Good thing you thought to blackmail me into coming." Gentleness lived in her voice, and that surprised him too.

"I did not think Father should go until daylight without treatment." Jonah shifted, stepped into the pool of light spilling from the room.

"I am no medical doctor, but you're right." She stood from the bed, a rustle of homespun skirts and grace. "Your father is very ill. I have applied a poultice to his chest to help clear his lungs. I shall leave a mixture. Someone will need to tend him, clean his chest in two hours, and apply more."

She had to tilt her face to meet his gaze. Why, 'twas a shame how fatigue rimmed those solemn blue eyes like bruises. As Tessa stepped closer, he wondered how hard her grandfather worked her and how many nights she crept alone into the forest.

Then his gaze landed on her woven basket packed with tiny sacks and crocks and the work-reddened hands gripping the handle. Tessa Bradford, despite her disagreeable personality, worked too hard for her living.

"Would you stay and see to it?" Jonah rubbed his brow and winced as his hand found a small bump at his temple "I have not slept the past two nights."

Neither had she. Tessa gripped the worn handle more tightly, uncertain how to handle this man. Bigger than legend, he was, and twice as handsome. How he could turn a sensible woman's head with that pleading lift of his single dark brow.

"Grandfather will not allow me to stay," she said now. "I have chores to tend to before meeting."

"I will speak to your grandfather."

"Nay. You are this man's son. You are able and strong and healthy." Her gaze roamed over the breadth of his shoulders, down the magnificent plane of his chest. My, how she remembered the feel of that chest when he'd held her. "You tend him."

Jonah's mouth curved into a lopsided grin "I will pay you twice what you deserve."

"You cannot buy me, Hunter." Tessa fought the urge to smile

back at him. Aye, it was doubly hard fighting off his charm. "Besides, I charge nothing for my services."

Nor was it right to charge the infirm and dying, trading pence for her knowledge of herbs and roots. But a man like Jonah Hunter, who would buy the whole town five times over, would never understand. To a man such as he, money was everything.

"And what will your grandfather say when he learns you have all but spent the night in my home, above stairs in a bedchamber?" Wicked eyes teased her. Eyes of a man so dashing, he could take her breath away if she let him.

"Try to charm me all you want, Hunter. It will not work."

"And if I should try harder?"

"Aye, go ahead. I know what you are about, you scoundrel. You are just trying to charm me into doing what you will not." Tessa lifted her chin and her basket, wondering how on earth she was to leave if his big, solid body blocked the threshold. "Your poor father, left with such a son."

She'd only meant to tease him in return. But the light faded from his eyes and the grin from his jaunty mouth. His shoulders squared, and she regretted her words. She had not meant to be unkind.

"I shall see you home, Mistress Tessa," he said now, formally, turning heel with military precision, all wickedness gone from his face.

Sadness crept down her spine. She felt as if she had caught a glimpse of the legendary Jonah Hunter no one in this town knew.

He walked away, his footsteps knelling in the cold stairway, and a lump formed in her throat.

Disappointment Well she knew the weight of that label, had worn it around her neck for as long as she could remember. The disappointing daughter, the disappointing relation with a hand out, always needing charity. Whose work in one relative's household after another was never good enough, never fast enough, never satisfactory.

Amazing. She and Jonah Hunter with his fine clapboard house and worldly possessions had this in common.

As her foot lighted on the last step and the warm heat from the parlor's hearth rushed at her face, she saw him stride across the room toward her. He held something dark in hand.

"Since you do not accept payment, then let me offer this." He held out the dark gray wool, folded precisely, the fabric so fine she took a step back. "Yours was ruined by the wolf."

"A cloak." Tessa spoke the words with wonder, but she would not reach out. She longed to touch that fine wool. But it was wrong. " 'Tis beautiful."

"This was my mother's." The bleak note that lowered his voice made her look up, forced her to see the emptiness in his eyes. "Not my stepmother, you remember her. But my real mother. She died when I was very young."

"You should keep such a fine remembrance."Tessa's throat tightened. "Such a thing is far too fine for the likes of me."

"Nonsense." Jonah shook out the folds of wool.

Why, she had never seen a cloak so beautiful. There was a pattern of checks to the wool, so dark and carefully woven. To own such a thing would be marvelous.

And what would her grandfather say? What would everyone else say? Wouldn't they laugh and wonder if poor spinster Tessa Bradford was holding out hopes for the man who had given her something so exquisite?

She had heard enough taunting and cruel remarks over the years. Her grandfather would probably take the garment from her anyway.

"You saved my life. That was payment enough." Tessa tried to smile, yet felt her chin wobble. She was no good at lying. And probably no good at hiding the liking she felt for that cloak.

"I will come by later today to check on your father," she said stiffly, forcing herself to move away from tempting Jonah Hunter and the beautiful cloak he held. "Keep him home from meeting and make sure he is warm. He must not take a chill."

"Tessa, I warrant the cloak is old." Jonah looked pained. Even disappointed.

Then she knew he meant only kindness in offering her such a gift, a payment for risking her grandfather's wrath and for tending his father. But she could not accept it.

"The cloak is precious and I would love it more than anything, but it is not meant for me, Jonah. 'Tis something you should save for the wife everyone is saying you have come home to choose."

He blushed. The wicked, outrageous rogue of a man turned pink from his collar to his ears. Aye, he was human after all. Tessa bit back a chuckle, knowing any friendliness between them was foolish. He would marry one of the pretty young girls from the village, but not her. Never her.

Her gaze strayed to the window where daylight shone through a scattering of pewter clouds. Her heart squeezed. "The sooner I am home, the better. Grandfather is . . ." she paused. "Strict"

Jonah winced and began carefully folding the beloved cloak. "I shall take you home."

"I have no need of an escort"

"Aye, but perhaps you will come across another wolf and need rescuing." A small light teased his eyes, but there was so much sadness there.

Tessa looked away, refusing to see the man inside. "Do not try to fool me, Jonah Hunter. You are the wolf, and I shall do my best to avoid you."

He barely managed a nod. There was no smile and no wicked laughter in his eyes as he continued folding the cloak. Carefully, the way a loving son might.

"Besides, once Grandfather sees I have disobeyed him, there will be no man on this earth able to rescue me. Good day to you, Jonah Hunter."

She turned to the door, refusing to think of the man greater than myth, the man who'd fought for the colonies, saved lives and farms with honor and courage. Everyone knew the stories, for Colonel Hunter, Jonah's father, spoke of it often enough that the boys around town lived on the stories.

How would the legend take to living an ordinary life, Tessa wondered as she headed out in the snow. How would a hero become an ordinary man?

CHAPTER THREE

"Thankful Bowman is an awful pretty girl. 'Course she is a little long in the tooth, but since she does not often smile, a man would not notice so much."

Jonah slammed his fist on the table, rattling silverware, fighting a suffocating panic. "Enough. I never said I *wanted* a wife."

On the other side of the cider pitcher, his unmanageable younger brother, hardly more than twenty, howled. "Surely, Jonah. Tell that to Father. He has done nothing more than talk of your homecoming for the last five years and of the wife you will take."

"I did not come home all this while because I knew what he wanted. Marriage is a trap I would rather avoid." The weight of his promise now tightened about his throat like a hanging noose. The idea of marriage was not a comforting one.

"So, you will break your vow to Father?"

Jonah felt his chest turn cold and it grew difficult to breathe. "Nay, I warrant this is a promise I'll keep."

As much as he wanted to run for freedom, Jonah knew he'd come home for good. With Father nearing the end of his days, there was naught he could do but fulfill the dying man's final wishes. He loved his father, and marriage was his duty. No matter how distasteful, Jonah vowed to find a bride.

Andy gulped down a great amount of cider before digging into his huge bowl of corn pone. "Why, every female in town has talked of little else for months. They seem to think you would make a fine catch, Jonah."

Thomas, the middle brother and more practical than salt, shook his head and helped himself to two more biscuits. " 'Tis true. A smart maiden has taken a good look at this house and figured how fine it would be to live here. Of course, once those maids get a good eyeful of our ugly brother, they will likely change their minds."

"Ugly?" Jonah roared. "Who in blazes are you calling ugly?"

His brothers laughed, and Jonah shook his head. "I will have no more talk of brides today."

"Brother, bellow orders at someone who'll listen." Andy wiped his brow. "If I was not mistaken, I heard a woman's voice in the hallway this morning, quite early too, just as the sun was rising. Have you been sowing oats your first night back in town?"

"Sowing oats? There is not a wench this side of Boston who will have him," Thomas declared gravely. There was more laughter.

Jonah grabbed his spoon and dug into his pudding, unable to stop thinking of the woman Andy had mentioned. He saw flashes of Tessa's face, made so tender and vulnerable in the lamplight, and jeweled blue eyes filled with sadness as she walked away from this house not an hour before.

At first Jonah feared the fine cloak didn't meet with her approval, an old piece of wool nearly thirty years old. But there was no mistaking the want in her eyes. Aye, Tessa Bradford coveted the garment he'd offered, but she'd walked away wearing nothing more than a coarse and faded homespun dress to protect her against the wind.

Truly a mystery. Jonah had met never a female who would refuse a man's gift, especially finery she didn't have. *You cannot buy me, Hunter.* Tessa's words haunted him.

"See? There *was* a woman in his room last night," Andy accused. "And he's smitten by her, too."

Jonah studied the amused light in his brother's eyes, read the interest and the delight "I am bound to disappoint you, little brother. There was no woman in my bed. Just Tessa Bradford come to tend Father."

The glee died from the room. Thomas cleared his throat, as if uncomfortable with the thought of one so severe as Mistress Bradford in the house at all. "She is a capable healer, no doubt. A sickness went through the village last winter, and half the children would be dead if not for her herbs and such."

"She scares me," Andy ruefully admitted as he spooned more corn pudding into his mouth. "Rumor was Horace Walling is thinking of marrying her."

"Horace Walling?" Jonah roared. "What kind of cruelty is a rumor like that? He was a wife-beating drunkard ten years ago when I left this town. I doubt he has changed his ways."

"Aye," Thomas agreed, dark eyes somber. "He has twelve children to care for since his last wife died in childbed before Thanksgiving."

And that was to be Tessa's fate? Rage burst through Jonah's chest, but he checked it in time. Hell, it was not his concern if she married some no good drunkard. Jonah had his own problems, even if his conscience nagged him.

"I shall stay home and tend Father today," he ordered, reaching for the pitcher. "You two bachelors can go to meeting and terrify all those pretty young maidens with your ugly faces."

"Not likely, big brother." Thomas cracked an uncommon grin. "Every marriageable female in this town will be done up in their finest, sitting expectantly on those meeting house benches waiting for the first sight of Major Jonah Hunter, town hero. Andy and I would be a sore disappointment to them."

"Speak for yourself, Thomas," Andy teased. "I would like to see all those beautiful young females for myself. Besides, Jonah may need my help in fighting them off. He knows plenty about Indians, but not one thing when it comes to handling a woman."

" 'Tis true," Jonah sighed. "I have given my word to Father, so there is no going back. Andy, come with me to today's meeting. Protect me from all those dangerous women."

He'd meant to joke, but sobered when neither brother laughed.

Sure enough, every unmarried girl from miles around crammed the hard board pews. Jonah froze in the aisle, shoulders braced, unabashedly terrified by the expectant shine in so many female eyes.

"They have not yet fainted from the sight of your ugly face." Andy nudged him in the side. "Wait, there is one wobbling a bit."

"Mayhap she got a good whiff of your feet." Jonah felt the weight of all those eyes, saw all the beribboned hats and dresses and nearly fainted himself.

One face after the other blurred in his mind, and a sick horror gripped him. Sweat broke out on his brow. How did one just pick a wife? There were so many young women. Why, they must be half his age. What did Father expect him to do? Wed a mere child?

A bad, bad feeling grew as he led the way down the aisle. Whispers rose with each step he took. He felt expectation rise like fog above a river. They thought him a war hero, thought him brave for killing savages. The truth clawed at his heart and he could not bring himself to meet one gaze or to focus on a familiar face, perhaps an old friend, and smile.

"No woman has lost consciousness so far," Andy reported as they settled onto the family pew.

"I swear it would be better for me if they did," Jonah whispered. The sharpness of so many gazes arrowed into his back. He couldn't remember the last time he felt this uncomfortable.

"Scared, big brother?"

"Aye." Jonah forced a swallow past his too-tight throat. "If they all fainted, I would be saved from having to marry."

"They would revive, dear brother, and then you would be no better off." Andy folded his hat in two. "Mayhap it is best just to pick one. Toss a coin or something. All women are just about the same in my opinion."

"Aye, that they are." Jonah thought of his stepmother and shuddered. Selfish to the core, that one. Were all marriages like that? Already dreading the bickering and the constant demands, he dared to turn a fraction and gaze about the church.

The back of a woman's head caught his eye. A white cap neatly hid the luxurious beauty of her hair, but tiny ringlet wisps peaked out from beneath the cap, dark silk against the white satin of her neck. She wore no cloak in this unheated meetinghouse. Why, 'twas so cold frost gleamed along the inside walls.

Tessa Bradford. He remembered the sight of her tending Father, the gentle caring of her hands, the softness in her face as she sat unguarded, unaware he was watching.

"Too sharp of tongue," Andy whispered. "And she is kind of ugly."

"No, she is just plain." Jonah remembered the light in her eyes, unique and compelling. She'd gone without sleep to tend Father, she'd walked away from a fine cloak when she had none. Nay, there was no ugliness, no selfishness to that one.

"Headstrong," Andy argued. "Now, her cousin is a beauty."

"Her cousin is half my age," Jonah ground out. Were there no other women over twenty years in this village?

"Well, the only other woman even nearly as ancient as you is the Widow Hawkins. She would be tolerable if a man could look past her warts."

"Andy, when I need your comments about a woman, I will ask." Jonah forced his gaze to the pulpit when the reverend cleared his throat. "Sensible. That is what I need. A sensible, undemanding woman."

"Pretty," Andy whispered as the sermon began.

Pretty? The place was packed full of pretty women with ambitious mamas. Jonah managed a forced grin when Charity Bradford, Tessa's stepgrandmother, cast him a huge smile. The blond girl seated next to her turned to smile too. But he wasn't dazzled.

Too many choices, and none of them what he wanted. Hell, he didn't want a wife. How could he? He'd lost his heart long ago when he'd taken his first step on the battlefield.

The tale of the wolves had grown to gargantuan proportion. Larger than life, the story grew—Jonah battling nearly a dozen wolves with his lone musket and saving the skating boys.

Of course the boys walked rather stiffly today, no doubt from angry spankings, but punishment hadn't dimmed the admiration shining in their youthful eyes, nor the tale itself.

Tessa listened with fear raw in her throat as her young cousin, a boy no more than ten, repeated the legend for the family. To her relief, no woman was mentioned. No one remembered or noticed her presence there that night.

Not that it mattered now. Grandfather had found a way to punish her. He'd finally found a way to rid his house of her presence. And she'd made matters much worse this morning, when he'd been scolding her like a five-year-old in the stable as she hurried her chores, by asking who would do all the work if she left? Not his lazy wife or his useless daughters, that was for certain. Grandfather had turned a frightening shade of purple and if she hadn't the pitchfork firmly in hand, Tessa knew without a doubt the cruel old man would have struck her.

Yes, her temper had made the situation much, much worse. And all because of Jonah Hunter and his bold arrogance. True, his father had needed her help desperately and he'd been right in coming for her, yet the truth remained. Had he not insisted that she leave the stable, she would have been home for her chores and no one would have noticed her absence or found the wet cloak in the cow pen.

"He's a dream," Violet murmured to her friend Thankful Bowman. "Too good to be true."

Tessa clenched her jaw as she finished clearing up the packed meal. A dream? Jonah Hunter was a decent woman's nightmare.

"And he has the most gorgeous house," Thankful sighed, shaking her blond curls just enough so that a carefully curled lock tumbled into her eyes. "The finest house from here to Boston."

"And servants," Violet sighed. "Yes, Major Hunter is an absolute dream."

Tessa fitted the lid on the crock and nearly threw it into the basket. Major Hunter, indeed. Call the man anything respectable, it didn't change the arrogance inside.

"Good afternoon, Ely." A deep voice broke through her malicious thoughts.

Both girls gasped. Tessa's fingers lost control and a knife tumbled from her grip.

Dark eyes met hers, laughing. "Let me fetch that for you, Mistress Tessa."

"I am perfectly capable," she argued, bending as he did. They knelt together beside the board table, the sunlight behind him covering her with his shadow.

" 'Tis the gentlemanly thing to do." His fingers snatched up the battered knife before she could.

"You are no gentleman, Hunter. A devil in a fine cloak, and no, you do not fool me. You may be able to impress a sixteen-year-old girl, but I have seen enough to know the type of man you are."

An amazing grin curved his mouth. "What type of man am I, mistress?"

"The kind that could benefit from the blunt end of a stick." Tessa grabbed the wooden handled knife from his big, fine-cut fingers.

"For shame!" Grandfather bellowed as he paced to a halt

behind her. A cold wind shivered along her skin. "Insulting our guest. Major Hunter, I feel I must apologize for my granddaughter's horrible behavior."

Jonah climbed to his feet, unfolding his powerful body with an easy grace. "Feel no need to excuse Tessa. I remember her quite well from my school days."

"Little has changed." Ely shook his head. "Good of you to make your way to our table. We have enough time for a cup of tea before the afternoon sermon starts. Will you share a cup?"

Jonah tugged at his collar. The nervous gesture made him look like a thief ready for hanging. "I have my brother to look after."

"He is a grown man," Tessa spoke, reaching inside the basket. "Sit, Hunter. Certain members of my family are anxious to hear how you shot so many wolves with a single musket"

She watched heat darken his face. So, almighty Jonah Hunter could be embarrassed after all. Well, let him be. He was preening before the women like a prize bull.

" 'Tis nothing but a tale," Jonah answered, dismissing the story grown into fiction with a wave of his well-formed hand. "Thank you for the tea, Mistress Tessa."

His fingers brushed hers as he took the simple wooden cup. Tiny flames danced up her arm. Appalled, she stepped away.

"He does not fancy you, Tessa," Violet whispered loud enough for everyone to hear.

Jonah's dark eyes landed on hers, his gaze as dazzling as the first star of the night Heavens, she could not look away. Grandfather's wife tittered, made some comment Tessa didn't even listen to. She ought to bow her head, tear her gaze from his, so arrogant Jonah Hunter could not see the pain in her heart. But she could not.

He broke the gaze, turning his sizzling eyes to Violet, blushing prettily in the midday sun. A dimple framed her smile, and to Tessa's despair, Jonah Hunter smiled back.

"I will take some of that sugar." His rich voice caressed the words.

Tessa shivered and turned away. She concentrated too hard on the task of pouring tea and serving it around the table. Her hands shook and she nearly spilled twice, but she ignored her stepgrandmother's scolding.

Why did she let him affect her so? Because he was so

handsome? Because he made her blood heat? Angry with herself, Tessa turned her back on him and tidied up.

"Hello, Ely. Mistress Tessa." A man's voice, rude and harsh, broke through the family's pleasant conversation.

"Horace," Ely welcomed.

Tessa's blood froze. She looked up into the haggard, lined face of her grandfather's neighbor. Watery eyes focused on her. A slow smile stretched his chapped lips.

"I have come to see my bride-to-be." His voice felt as cold as ice. "I want to walk her back to the meetinghouse."

Tessa took one step back and into the table. Boards rattled. A crock thumped in protest. A man's big hand covered her elbow. She looked up, and Jonah stood at her side, wide shoulders set, his powerful body tensed.

"Bride-to-be?" he roared. "What the devil is he talking about?" A muscle jumped in Jonah's square jaw. "Tessa, explain to me what Walling means?"

Little fires licked her skin trapped beneath the heat of his hand. Her heart raced as fast as a bird in flight. Tessa felt dizzy, unable to breathe, as Horace stepped forward and held out one unwashed, bone-thin hand.

"I—" She swallowed, unable to say the words. It felt as if her heart died looking at the unkempt man in the doorway. In the common yard beyond, she saw families packing up their dinners and heading back to the meetinghouse, wives beside their husbands, children huddling around them.

"Horace has agreed to marry my granddaughter and take her out of my household for good." There was no mistaking the pride in Ely Bradford's voice. He clearly didn't want Tessa. Was proud he'd done little better than force her on a brutal husband.

Jonah's throat tightened. Anger beat at his chest. She felt so fragile beneath his hand. He felt fine bone and sinewy muscle. She was lean and spare, too damn lean in his opinion. Looking at her face, so sad, lined with fatigue, it didn't take a genius to know why.

Ely worked her harder than most would work a slave. And treated her worse, too. Why, she had nothing to ward off the last of the winter's harsh winds. Only a thin woolen shawl, ragged and worn.

"Let Major Hunter come to know Violet better," Ely dared to say now, "and go with Horace, Tessa. Oh, and take the dirty dishes with you."

He felt Tessa tense, her muscles drawing up ready to fight. Then she moved from his touch. She stepped away, a slim ribbon of a thing, picking up cups and gathering spoons with quiet efficiency.

Jonah's chest tightened when she folded the basket shut and took one halting step toward Horace Walling. The foul bastard grinned, exposing yellowed, rotten teeth. Anger roared through Jonah's blood.

"She is the worst tempered female in the colony," Charity Bradford began in her irritating, overly gracious tone. "Thank goodness Violet is sweet tempered. Please, do not think such horrid character runs in the blood."

One look at Violet's calculating, greedy eyes told Jonah the girl was far from sweet. Words of protest rose in his throat, words to defend Tessa from these people who called themselves family, but he stopped.

He remembered how Tessa had walked away from him this morning in the parlor, how she'd refused his help, called him wolf, told him he could not buy her. There was no selfish want in her eyes, no coveting a fine home. Hell, she hadn't even wanted the payment he'd offered.

A small light of admiration burned in his chest Not that he found Tessa Bradford attractive. No. A woman with such a sharp tongue could slice a man in two.

And yet she was one woman who—

No, he would not think it Tessa was to be married. She was too old, too difficult, too stubborn, and Andy was right. She wasn't pretty.

He bid the family goodbye, startled by Violet's sultry smile. What was wrong with this child? And with the others half his age looking at him as if he could move the moon, as if he were a hero?

Bleakness beat at his heart. When they looked at him, could they not see it? He was nothing but a man. A man of flaws and fears and a heart that had died long ago.

He did not want a sixteen-year-old for a wife. He wanted a woman, one strong enough to stand beside him, one who wasn't afraid of work.

Jonah's gaze landed on Tessa, trudging silently beside pole-thin Horace Walling, her head bowed, defeat weighing down her shoulders.

"Do not even think it, brother," Andy advised, hurrying to catch him.

Jonah laughed aloud. "How do you know what I am thinking?"

"You are thinking of duty. And well you should." Little brother clasped him hard on the shoulder. "I am just back from the house. Father is failing. Thomas said to bring Mistress Tessa at once."

Fear froze Jonah. He felt his blood stall in his veins. His own legs refused to move. "What? Is Father dying so soon?"

"I don't know." Andy's face turned grim, his eyes bleak. True sorrow burned there. "But you had best pick one of those women now, brother. If the old man does not improve, this well might be your last day as a bachelor."

CHAPTER FOUR

" 'Tis not good news," she spoke from the thick shadows of the room.

Jonah stood, his heart quickening. Fear tasted sour in his mouth. Tessa Bradford stepped farther into the parlor, the few lit candles stroking her face with alternating ribbons of darkness and light.

"Tell me. I need to know the truth," he demanded.

"His lungs are failing." She pushed a handful of ebony ringlet curls out of her regret filled eyes. Eyes that touched him with sympathy. "Jonah, I have done my best to ease his discomfort, but you must call a surgeon. There is naught more I can do."

"Then do more." Jonah tore across the room, knocking aside a chair. Anger tore at his chest—the only feeling he'd known for so long—and it raged bright enough to burn him clear through. "Father cannot die. You must do something. Get back upstairs. Use your herbs—"

She raised two slender hands, callused, work-reddened. "Jonah, I cannot—"

"Do it, I say!" Anger ground his words into a threat. His fingers closed around her upper arms, holding her captive, hostage to the emotions tearing him apart. "You cannot let Father die."

"Jonah." Her soft voice, nearly whispering his name, stopped him, made him blink. The red rage before his eyes ebbed. He saw

Tessa's heart-shaped face, lined with fatigue, crinkled with worry. Tears shimmered in her eyes. "You're bruising me."

In shock, he let her go. She took a step back, rubbing her small hands over her forearms, as if to chase away his touch. Or the crushing pain from his grip.

Shame filled him. He'd never hurt a woman. Would never wish to— He hung his head. "Tessa, I'm sorry."

"No matter." Cold and distant, she sounded. Strangely disappointed. "You're overwrought, I understand. The news is not good. I plan to stay and do what I can. Regardless of what you think of me, I would never leave a dying man alone and suffering."

A dying man. Her words struck him like a blow. Damn fool, he'd been gone too long. He'd let the years slip by like dirt through his fingers, never stopping to think his father, so strong and brave, would not live forever. Jonah took a step back, mind reeling.

And now, was he too late? Would there be no time to share tales, watch sunrises, walk the cornfields with Father and speak of harvests, of hopes for the future?

He had no one to blame but himself. In chasing after what he'd hoped would make Father proud, he'd lost a decade, precious time that could not be recovered.

A pair of velvet blue eyes gazed up at him, shimmering with unshed tears and an emotion that drew him hard and fast. Air lodged in Jonah's chest seeing the hurt he'd caused. A hurt he could not guess at.

"I'm sorry, Tessa." The words came broken, edged with defeat. He'd been wrong to raise his voice and to hold her captive. "I know you have done all you can."

Her bottom lip wobbled. Soft and full, too lush for her thin, pale face. " 'Tis all right."

Yet she turned away, shoved her callused hands deep in her faded skirt's pockets and ascended the stairs. Blood thickened in his veins watching the sway of her hips beneath her skirt. The darkness swallowed her until there was only the sound of her light foot on the steps.

Jonah rubbed his hands over his face. Aye, always the fool. If he were half as successful in relationships, in interacting with other people as he'd been on the battlefield . . . Well, that was his true failure. Something he could not hide here in this house, in this small town, where family and relationships were everything.

"Was that Mistress Tessa I heard?" Thomas' voice came from the shadowed library. "Has she good news of Father's condition?"

"Nay." Only two candles flickered against the darkness. Jonah hadn't the heart to light more. Now he saw only the shadow of his brother, broad shouldered and far more capable than he himself could ever be. "He is ailing. I am off to fetch a surgeon from Saybrook. Tell Andy. Tessa will need help if Father worsens."

" 'Tis foolish for you to leave." Thomas stepped into the ribbons of light, solemn eyes unflinching. "I will go after a doctor."

"Nay, I shall do it—"

"I have been here these last few years, Jonah. I can spare the time away from him. You cannot."

Shame crept around his heart and squeezed like a grip. "I must go." He reached for his cloak.

"I know the way best." Thomas' hand stopped him. "Night will come before long, and I can find my way better than you through the dark. I have traveled the roads more. Trust me, Jonah, I will ride faster and return more quickly. 'Twill be best for Father."

" 'Tis only sensible." Shame tightened its grip inside his chest. "Thank you, brother. I will find Andy and carry in more firewood. Make myself useful somehow."

"You are too harsh with yourself. It can be no easy task trying to fill Father's footsteps. Do not try so hard to be somebody else." Thomas' voice dipped, and kindness shone in his eyes. "I will saddle one of the stallions and leave immediately."

"Godspeed, brother." Jonah listened to Thomas' steps in the kitchen, heard the back door bang shut, felt silence creep through the house.

He heard the slightest footfall on the ceiling above. Tessa. Until the surgeon came, Father's fate lay in her caring hands.

She recognized Jonah's step in the hallway. She only had time to brace herself before he strolled through the door, all brash and spellbinding brawn.

"You look exhausted." Kindness flickered in his compelling eyes.

Little bubbles of heat popped in her blood. Why did she react strongly to him? He made her think of her most secret dreams, of how good his body had felt against hers, hard and strong and so wondrously male. She opened her mouth, but no words came.

"Any change?" Jonah demanded from the threshold, his voice tight.

"Nay."

"You're angry at me." He winced. "Because I hurt you. I didn't mean it. I didn't know I was bruising you."

Of course not. He'd held her with a possessive strength she'd never felt before, claiming and unyielding and filled with heart-deep need. No one had ever held her that way. No one ever would again.

"You need not worry," she said quietly, folding the used towel in careful thirds. "I know that there is not a single man alive who would hold me on purpose."

She'd meant it as a small joke, but no humor shaped his grim, well-shaped mouth.

"Mayhap you should stop doing your best to scare off all the men." His gaze bore into hers, glimmering with knowledge.

"I do no such thing." She jumped up from the low bedside stool so fast she nearly knocked it to the ground. "Just because I do not dally with every available man, the way you do with women, does not mean—"

"Do you think I like being forced to marry?" In three strides he'd crossed the room.

"Forced?" She knelt before the fire, hating that she now gazed at his booted feet. "Your father wants grandchildren. I hardly call that having a gun to your head."

"To me it is the same."

"Then you live too easy of a life." Forced to marry? The dolt knew nothing. Living in a fine house, a hero in his family's eyes, so handsome any woman would fall at his feet and be honored to feel his love. "No one is threatening to toss you out if you do not marry."

Silence. Perhaps he would leave now, go so that she need not see him and fight memories of his rock hard chest, so male and so fascinating. And how amazing it felt simply to be touched by a man, by him.

Truly, a foolish thought. He'd held her and it meant nothing to him. There would be no man to love her. No family of her own built on happiness and trust.

She lifted a stick of chopped maple from the ornate brass wood box, something far too fine for holding a stack of wood.

Big fingers curled around her own. Beautiful, blunt-tipped

fingers that snapped heat through her bones. Tessa's blood warmed as Jonah knelt beside her and lifted the wood from her grip.

"Allow me." His voice could caress all common sense from a woman.

"I will allow you nothing." She released the wood, hoping he would release her hand. He did. He'd meant nothing by touching her. Why did she feel so disappointed? "We are nearly out of wood."

Dark eyes sizzled, drawing her closer. "My brother is bringing more."

"Aye, I'm not surprised." Tessa stood, determined to keep her distance. "A hero such as yourself is too important to carry an armload of wood."

"That is not what I meant—"

"I doubt you know what a good day's work feels like. No, hard labor is beneath Major Jonah Hunter." Anger felt easier than admitting what was truly bothering her, what was ripping her heart in two.

"I never said I was so fine," he ground out. "The damn truth is—"

"You have every girl in town pining after you, batting her eyes, trying to win your favor. And look at you, soaking it up when your father is so gravely ill." What right did he have complaining about having to marry? How dare he complain when he could have what she would not?

"That is not true and you know so, Tessa."

"I know nothing. Do you think I will melt at your feet the way Violet and her friends did?"

His eyes sizzled. "I doubt you would melt for any man, Tessa Bradford."

His hand clamped on her wrist, and her breath wedged in her throat. His bare skin scorched hers, the heat absorbing into her body.

Why was she behaving this way? Was she so desperate for his touch that she would imagine Jonah Hunter as a man capable of giving love? Anger tore at her.

"I'm too wise to melt for a man. Especially a handsome one." She fetched a clean washcloth from a pile of linen.

"So, you think me handsome?"

She clenched the cloth in her fist. "I do not," she lied. "But I bet that you think yourself handsome. And admit it, you liked how those young girls flocked around you, simpering for your attention."

"I don't give a damn for those girls playing dress up and thinking that I am some tasty meal ticket," he ground out, fury so tight in his jaw he could barely form the words.

"Now, you are lying."

Fire burned in his eyes. "Nay, I'm telling the truth. I hardly care what you think of me. You're in this house to tend Father, not render judgment on me. Is that clear?"

"I am not one of your indentured servants, bought and paid for, so don't treat me as if I am." Her fingers trembled from fatigue, surely not emotion, as she rung moisture from the cloth. "I may not be pretty and young, but at least I'm not like those ridiculous girls hoping to be your bride."

"Tell me how you are smarter, Tessa." His shadow fell across her, claiming her as swiftly as his touch.

Her skin burned. Her blood tingled. Was there no stopping her body's response to him? "I am not fooled by a man's false heart. Especially a man thinking of his earthly needs when his father is lying so ill."

"What know you of a man's earthly needs?" His voice boomed through the room, echoing off the papered walls.

Tessa blushed. "Hand me the towel over there, please. Jonah, I shall have no more—"

"A woman such as you must know a lot about a man such as I," he interrupted, his big body so near to hers she could feel the power thrumming through his tensed muscles.

"Jonah, keep your voice down. Your father is fast asleep." Heavens, she should not have risked his temper.

His teeth ground, clacking together. "I will not. I want to know about you, so strict and pious on the outside, but I know differently. How dare you judge me as if I were mere mud at your feet?"

"I never said you were mud," she protested and tried to step away. His hand caught her, held her close. Way too close to that solid wall of his chest.

"Tell me what you were doing in the woods last night? What foul business were you about? I think I have a clue. Since you know so much about a man's earthly needs, then mayhap you've been tending to them."

Heat popped across her skin as he closed the distance between them. He dipped his face toward hers. She stumbled back. He caught her by the elbows, his firm grip twice as possessive and as unyielding as before. Was there no escape? Jonah leaned closer. The breath stalled in her chest. She tried to protest, but his lips claimed hers in a burst of heat and velvet and possession. Heat swept across the surface of her lips where their mouths joined. Hot, bubbling pleasure that somehow twisted low in her stomach.

Sweet heaven. Tessa melted against him. He was all rock-solid muscle and powerful man, but his mouth brushed hers with such surprising tenderness that she could not move.

"You taste sweeter than you look," he murmured.

She tasted his every word, every breath. Jonah's hand curled around her neck, cradling the back of her head. Heat pulsed in her blood as his lower lip caught hers and sucked it into his mouth. Sweet Mary, she'd never known such scorching heat. Never known such a touch. Was Jonah Hunter such a man that he could bring fire to her cold heart?

His tongue brushed velvet heat along the seam of her lips. This was like a kiss she'd dreamed of on those unhappy nights when she lay unable to sleep in her bed. This kiss was like a dream, and it sizzled like magic wonder along her lips, fired her blood, and made her bones melt. Overcome, Tessa laid her hand against his jaw and felt the curious texture of his unshaven whiskers, wondrous and rough against her palm.

Was this a dream? Tessa did not know as his arms folded her to his chest. She felt the strength of him and the powerful beat of his heart. Thrilling pleasure spun through every inch of her. A pleasure that made her feel alive and whole and so miraculously wanted. Even as desire filled her veins, it did not distort her reasoning. Jonah Hunter didn't want her, she knew that. She ought to step away and move out of his embrace.

And yet as his kiss grew more demanding and his mouth harder and faster over hers, she surrendered, melting like frost before sun. Nothing in her quiet sensible life had ever felt like this. And considering she was the most feared spinster in the village, she knew without a doubt she would never be kissed like this again. So she was secretly glad when he did not move away. Just for this once she wanted to know the way a man touched a woman. Feel a passion she'd heard about in shy whispers from her few married friends.

"Tessa."

She felt his big body tense. Her entire body cooled when she met his gaze.

"I'm sorry," he murmured, releasing her, stepping away as if he'd touched something distasteful.

The old pain wrapped itself around her heart. No man was going to love her. She'd waited for love, believed in it for so long. All those years tending poor sick Mother, she dreamed it might be possible. One of the handsome men from town, one she saw at meeting. Sometimes a man would smile at or stop to exchange pleasantries on the common and her silly old heart would start hoping...

Aye, simple foolishness. She'd turned twenty-six this winter. Far too old to dream of romance and passion.

"I suppose now you think—" He sighed, raking his hair with one hand, long dark strands falling through his frustrated fingers.

"You cannot know what I think," she argued, far too embarrassed to meet his gaze. Want for him still sparked her blood.

"You think I would consider you—"

"I hate you, I truly do." She cut him off before he could say the hateful words. Nay, he would never consider marrying her. The hurt clutched her heart, such an old pain of being unwanted. "I would never want such a pompous ass for my husband."

"Believe me, I am no donkey, Tessa."

"Nay, you are worse." There was no such thing as love from a man with danger in his eyes. With her pulse thundering in her ears, she turned her back on him and steeled her heart. "I will need some fresh water."

"Tell me about your lover. He can't be Horace Walling. No woman would sneak through the night woods to meet with such a clod pate."

"You think that I—" She could not say it. Shock lodged in her throat.

"I know it," he corrected, eyes flashing. "No virgin kisses the way you do."

"But I—"

"Tell me," he demanded, towering over her powerful and bold, handsome enough to take her breath away and every last bit of her sense.

The memory of his kiss burned along her mouth. Dreams felt like that, fiery and heart stopping. Reality was different, disappointing and grim. The two could not mix. Hadn't she learned that by now?

"Tell you what?" Tears blurred her vision. His dark face swam, and she blinked. Two drops spilled down her cheeks, betraying her feelings. She would not let him see her vulnerable.

"Tell me where you learned to kiss like that," A grin whispered across his mouth, still glistening from their kiss.

It took all her willpower not to strike him. How dare he tease her? "You know damn well I have never kissed a man."

"Not even me, I suppose?" His dark brows drew taut. Muscles bunched along his whisker-rough jaw. "Do not tempt me, Tessa, else the entire village will know of your midnight adventures."

"Don't you dare." Her warning thrummed through her like hatred, hard and hot and terrifying.

"You start a rumor such as that, and you'll do more than ruin me."

"Mistress, you've done that on your own." His eyes narrowed, a devil's light glowing within.

"I despise you." She fetched a towel and tossed it at him. "You're not so fine a man as you think."

A wry grin twisted his mouth. "So, I was only good enough to save your life last night and convenient for you to tease with your experienced kisses?"

"You are nothing but a man of falsehoods, Hunter. You cannot hide that from me."

A thud ricocheted through the room. Tessa jumped. Jonah whirled. The youngest Hunter son stood in the threshold, surprise lighting his innocent brown eyes, a fallen chunk of wood at his feet.

"Thought you might need more wood for the fire," he croaked. "To keep Father warm."

When would she learn to keep her tongue? Andy Hunter now gazed at her as if she'd sprouted two heads. There was little wonder how she'd earned her reputation for being sharp-tongued. Jonah stood with an apology shimmering in his night-dark eyes.

"Yes, Andy, please bring in the wood." Wearily, Tessa eased down on the stool.

The youngest Hunter brother kept a wide distance from her as he stacked the sticks inside the fine brass container, then slipped from the room as if he expected her to cast a spell on him.

The old man lay breathing unevenly, but stable. He was holding his own. For now. Well, the poultice had cooled enough. She would clean off his chest and apply more. She could do little else until the surgeon came.

Aye, it would be best to keep her hands busy. Then she would not have to think about what she'd said, how she'd behaved. Shameful tears beat behind her eyelids. A lump thickened in her throat.

Jonah Hunter could tease her about her inexperience. It mattered little. He would find a pliable, pretty bride to make babies with. And she would be stuck in the marriage her grandfather had bought for her. Trapped in a nightmare she feared she might never wake from.

"She fell asleep about twenty minutes ago," Andy whispered, as if he were afraid to wake the notoriously sharp-tongued Tessa Bradford.

"I know." Jonah laid his hand over Father's. Heat buzzed at his fingers. The old man was much too hot.

Tessa had stacked cool, herb-scented compresses in a small washbasin, and he laid one across Father's brow before answering his brother. "Aside from a short trip home to fix her grandfather's family their supper, Tessa has been working here since midday without a single complaint. Look, 'Tis nearly midnight now."

Where the hell is Thomas with the doctor? Fear drummed inside him. Father was desperately ill. Jonah sensed it might already be too late.

Tessa stirred, slumped in the chair by the fireplace. Well, he had to admire how hard she worked. He alone knew she'd not slept two nights in a row, and had no leisure to nap in the day between. She worked beyond exhaustion tending Father, worrying over his fever, easing the old man's struggle for air.

Light shimmered in her black-as-silk hair and washed her face, softening the fatigue written around her mouth. He studied those lips, generous cut and sweeter than wine. Who knew spinster Tessa Bradford could turn a man inside out with her kiss? The blood in his groin thickened.

"How's Father?" Andy approached the bed, dread and grief

dark in his boyish eyes.

"Burning up." Jonah laid his hand against the old man's jaw. His skin felt too hot. His sleep was growing restless. "Damn it, Thomas should have returned by now. Where is that doctor?"

"Thomas is doing his best. I have no doubt about it."

"I should have gone." Anger smoldered in his chest like a long burning ember, flickering when exposed to air.

"That is right, big brother. You do everything bigger and better and faster than the rest of us." No accusation, but hard-edged truth sharpened Andy's voice. "Thomas is as capable as you. And he knows the night roads better. Does it pain you so much not to be the hero?"

A hero? Andy may speak truth, but he knew little of what was heroic. Nothing he'd done in the last ten years had been so, not facing death, not killing enemies of the Crown, not being responsible as men died beneath his command. Would his father die now?

"Let me spell you, Jonah." Tessa's voice came soft, sympathetic.

Perhaps she was tired. Or perhaps she'd overheard Andy's words. Jonah's chest tightened. Did this woman have to know so many of his secrets? That ember of anger flickered more brightly inside.

Yet one look at Tessa as she wove around the bedstead, her plain homespun skirts rustling with her graceful gait, drained away all his anger, all his shame. For one moment he saw compassion in her dark eyes so bright and tender.

The heat of her remembered kiss fanned across his mouth, firing his blood.

"Lie down." Her hand, small and warm, rested on his.

Then he thought about what it would be like to lie down with her. "I am not tired."

"There is no telling how long Thomas will take, and I can hear the danger in your father's breathing. Rest while you can. Surely, I will need your help later."

"How can I sleep?" The question tore through him, the guilt and concern and fear beating within his heart.

Swirls of black curls brushed her face. "I don't know. But try. Your father may soon need your strength."

Gratitude broke apart the lump in his throat. Tears, hot and painful, collected behind his eyes. How did this woman, so stubborn and difficult, understand? Perhaps for the same reason she tasted like heaven and fired want through his blood.

"I left a quilt on the chair." Tessa lifted her hand, stepped away, waiting to take his place on the low bedside stool. "Don't worry, Jonah. I will wake you if there are any changes."

He trusted her. This woman so hard-willed, so different from his notion of what a female should be. Desire licked down his spine at her nearness. Why hadn't he noticed it before? Such firm breasts, soft and full, drew his gaze, filling him with a heady want. If Father weren't so ill, he would reach out and touch them.

"Come, get some rest" Tessa smiled, vulnerable in the candlelight and oh, so soft.

"I might as well rest my eyes a bit," he agreed, rising, resisting the need to take her in his arms again. Was she bewitching him? And yet as he patted his Father's hand and crossed to the fire, he knew the truth.

He was terrified and she offered understanding, 'twas all. Father was dying. And he, as the oldest son, had failed him. He had not yet married. Did not wish to marry. How was he to trust a woman who coveted only his house, his money, any comfort he could give her? How was an honorable life built on so little?

As the crackling fire heated his back, Jonah watched Tessa spear poor Andy with her dark gaze.

"Fetch me another basin of cold water," she demanded. "Do it now."

Andy scrambled away, his eyes wide, more afraid of Tessa than of Father's dying. Who could blame the boy? She was frightening him on purpose, pretending she was a shrew when underneath her sharp words beat a gentle heart

Tessa's gaze snared his. Heat jumped in his loins. "I am afraid, too."

His worries were none of her business. She had no right seeing into his soul, no right measuring the fear inside the man.

Jonah settled into the single chair by the fire, fighting hard to control the jumble of feelings in his chest. Anger. Shame. Remorse. It mulled together, blending with such power he feared he would lose control.

When he finally closed his eyes, his last vision was of Tessa leaning over his father. He drowsed, listening to her movements, a rustle of muslin skirt, a splash of water, and the light rhythm of her breath.

"Jonah?"

He bolted up from the chair. Tiny creases shadowed the corners of her eyes. Fear darkened them.

That same fear beat in his heart. "What's happened?"

No sharp tongue, no stubbornly set chin. Only pure vulnerability as she clenched her hands together. "I thought you should know. I fear the end is near. I have sent Andy for the reverend."

CHAPTER FIVE

Tears of exhaustion burned behind her eyes, yet Tessa refused to stop working. The cold night wind burned her face, chilled her through to the bone, but she clutched the large washbasin in both hands and plunged it into the snow bank.

Beside her, Jonah did the same, a silent giant of a man who lifted a bucket of frozen snow and headed toward the house. He didn't look at her, but she would not wipe away the memory of his scorching kiss.

Heart hardened, Tessa followed Jonah's shadow in the moonless night, as afraid of his silence as what he may be thinking. Aye, she knew what he thought No man would want her. He even feared she was holding hopes that he would chose her for his bride.

She tried her best to ignore him. To concentrate on her work—a man's life was at stake—yet when she least expected it, there it was. Her gaze followed the sight of Jonah's strong shoulders or lingered on his hard-set mouth.

The old man's fever soared as minutes ticked by, his heart beating weak and far too fast. Sweat dripped off her own brow as she struggled up the narrow stairs and down the hall, following Jonah into the bedchamber.

The sight of his hands holding the snow-filled bucket made her heart stop, made her shamefully wonder what his touch, capable and sure and powerful, would feel like on other parts of her body.

She bowed her head, thankful Jonah refused to meet her gaze, and together they tucked snow around his father's frail body. The man murmured in his sleep, crying out in terror. The bucket tumbled from Jonah's grip and he dropped onto the stool close to the bedside, cradling the old man's hands within his.

Tessa's chest squeezed at the sight. A single candle brushed pulsing light across the back wall, leaving Jonah's profile in dark silhouette. Unafraid and solemn, he leaned close enough to his father to whisper low, comforting words. There was no mistaking the love in his voice, so rich and full.

Who knew Jonah Hunter could be so tender? So uncommon and good? She saw the tears shimmer where they fell against the quilt and knew he was grieving his father's suffering. She thought of the man in the tales, the warrior, the soldier, the leader of men, and knew that all his accomplishments paled next to this great act of loving and comforting his father.

For the first time she saw with her eyes the hero inside the man.

She left them, washbasin in hand, and hurried down the stairs, feeling insignificant next to the love Jonah had for his father. Such was a love she'd had for her mother, tending the poor ailing woman all those years when she should have been courting a man's interest, planning her wedding, and later, making babies.

Jonah Hunter was not so bad of a man. Nay, he was excellent. Arrogant and handsome and sly enough to charm the devil, but underneath his brashness, he was a man capable of loving.

The night wind burned her cheeks and hands, drafted through her skirts, and she shivered. Tessa knelt and scooped the basin full of frozen snow and dashed back to the house, scurrying through the unlit rooms and up the dark stairs.

When she burst into the room, Jonah glanced up. He looked to be nothing but shadow, but he was so much more. Substantial. Courageous. Her heart ached as she tucked the snow around the old man's side. Wordless, she turned and dashed away, fear driving her steps.

Had she done enough for Jonah's father? She did not know. Exhaustion slowed her movements and she fought it, pushed herself harder. Down the stairs, out into the snow, back up and into the room.

Up again and down again until tears filled her eyes. As the old man inched closer to death, she feared his breathing would halt entirely and she would be left with Jonah's grieving tears and the terrible sense she should have done more.

She laid her hand on the colonel's forehead. So damn hot. His breath came in rattling whispers. What more could she do? Tessa set down the basin, refused to meet Jonah's eyes, and hurried back downstairs. Perhaps another onion poultice would break apart the congestion in the old man's lungs. She would need a hot fire. Yet the kitchen was dark, and she tried twice to light a lamp in the corner. Pain burned in her back and coiled in her neck.

She thought of Jonah's quiet courage and pushed herself harder. How many bedsides had she sat beside, comforting a dying loved one when others would not? Death frightened a lot of people, but not Jonah. He sat vigil beside his father so that the old man would not die alone.

Admiration burned in her heart. Or maybe it was something greater. There was no fooling herself. She felt a deep attraction to the man. His touches, his kisses filled her dreams.

Such foolishness. She knelt before the hearth and uncovered the embers. A few light breaths had the coals glowing red. She added kindling and listened to it spark. Love should be like this, starting gently, growing and feeding onto itself until nothing could stop it.

Yet one needed a worthy man to love. Like Jonah Hunter. What a lucky woman his bride would be.

The back door flew open, banging against the wall, startling her. She dropped the stick of maple, and it clattered to the floor.

"I have brought the doctor," Thomas announced as he charged into the room, tearing off his wet, ice-ridden cloak. "Is Father—"

"Still alive," Tessa finished, rising from the floor, the fledging fire forgotten.

She blushed as the surgeon entered the room, a young man come from so far. What must he think? His smart blue gaze studied her fallen hair and her worn and stained garments. Tessa felt heat creep across her face.

Aye, she was no beauty, but what a sight she must look. And deep in her heart she dared to hope Jonah found her attractive? Ashamed, she lowered her gaze.

The men stormed through the room, leaving boot tracks of mud and snow to melt in their hurry. Her work was done now. Sadness filled her. She liked to be needed, yet the doctor would know how best to help the dying man.

Alone in the silent room, Tessa lifted her shawl from the back of the kitchen chair where she'd left it. She prayed the old Colonel Hunter would live. Now, there was nothing more to do but wait.

Should she leave? Ice fell from the black sky as she glanced out the small window, clinging to scratchy limbed trees. The world looked so desolate, as if already mourning this night. Nay, she would stay, as she would with any patient, Jonah Hunter and his effect on her be damned.

Tessa returned to the fireplace and added plenty of wood. She would heat water for tea. Thomas and the surgeon looked frozen through. Then she would wait with the family for the end. Perhaps she could somehow help ease the suffering for the old man.

And in the quiet hours, until they needed her again, Tessa vowed not to think of her future. By this time next week she would be married to Horace Walling, that is, if her grandfather had his way.

Swallowing tears, Tessa reached for the water bucket. Empty, of course. Jonah's cloak hung from a peg by the back door. She slid the fabric over her shoulders, so heavy and finely woven. The wool smelled clean and faintly of a midnight forest, the way he did.

She closed the door with a click. Light glowed from the upstairs window through the sheen of the ice storm. Cold wind whipped through her skirts, and inside she felt as bleak as that breeze.

Jonah's kiss still tingled on her lips, spellbinding. How he'd tasted of passion and teased her with a glimpse of what she could not have. There would be no passionate, tender love in her future. The pain in her heart broke in two and she stepped into the yard.

Ice battered her. She didn't feel it. She could not feel anything at all. She'd lost her dreams, the hopes that kept her alive. It was not an easy situation living with a family who begrudged her presence. At night, so tired she could not sleep, she would wish on the closest star for the one thing that mattered: a family of her own to love and care for. And who would love her in return.

Horace Walling's face blurred in her mind, haggard and narrow-eyed and frightening. Tessa shuddered, her dreams dying one by one.

She knelt before the well, vowing not to cry. But the tears came anyway.

"I brewed some tea," she whispered to Andy, slumped by the fire, face buried in his hands.

The young man looked up, tears in his eyes. Exhaustion and worry saddened his face. Just back from fetching the reverend, he was too troubled to remember to be frightened of her. "I'm much obliged, Mistress Tessa."

" 'Tis just tea." Boiling water was easy work next to the dilemma poor Andy faced. And yet, he could not see what she saw. Could not begin to appreciate that the years he'd already had with his father were a treasure greater than money or a fine home.

Her own father had died when she was a small girl. His face and even the sound of his voice had faded from her memory. But his happiness, the tenderness she'd felt when he cradled her in his lap before the fire and read to her from the great books he brought all the way from England, those memories remained. Faded by time, now they seemed no more than dreams.

No matter how hard her life had been since, Tessa always knew her father loved her. Losing him to a simple injury, aye, it never should have taken his life, changed hers forever. A broken arm wasn't so dangerous, yet there had been no one trained to set bones properly, to apply poultices to help the swelling and the bleeding. No one who knew more than mere home remedies for battling fever.

"My, that smells wonderful," the reverend hinted.

Tessa carried the fine silver tray across the room and held it steady while the silver-haired man poured milk into a steaming cup of tea.

"And biscuits too," he tried to smile.

That wobbly smile made Tessa's heart hurt all the more. She'd seen death more times than she could count and knew the signs, the feel of it in the room. She feared there would be no mercy this night.

"Jonah, you must eat," Thomas' voice boomed. Only the fire crackling in the hearth and ice tapping the glass window dared to make a sound.

"I am not hungry." Jonah did not turn from his place at the foot of his father's bed. Nor did he lift his solemn gaze from the old man's fevered face.

"Starving yourself will not change his condition."

Thomas' eyes warmed, the grief ebbing just enough for Tessa to see the gleam inside—a sight that made her throat close entirely.

Respect. Admiration. Love for his brother. She knew she shouldn't be observing a family's intimate warmth. Tessa ducked her chin as Thomas poured tea from the pot and handed it to Jonah.

There was no way she could get out of the pending marriage. The image of Horace Walling's face swirled before her. Her head spun. Pain cracked in her chest. Tessa set the tray on a small table, blinking hard, surprised such thoughts would intrude here, in this sick room where they did not belong. She had the surgeon to assist and, when he was gone, a patient to tend.

"Tessa." Jonah's hand reached out. Big fingers engulfed hers.

"Y-yes?" Fire from his touch streaked along her skin.

"I ought to thank you for the tea." Grief-darkened eyes that searched hers. "And for your help. 'Tis good to be home again. In a place where neighbors help one another."

She did not want him seeing her with tears in her eyes. She took a step back, and anger speared through her. He was such a stupid man. What did he think? She was here because they were neighbors? "I am not here to help you, Hunter. You are not the reason I am up for the second straight night without sleep."

"Of course not. My father—"

"That is right I am here for your father. For a man who is old and sick and who needs care."

"And I thank you for it."

So, even a man who thought himself heroic was as daft as the rest of them. "Don't you understand?"

"I know nothing of herbs."

"Herbs have naught to do with it." She fisted both hands and vowed not to give him a good smack that might knock some sense into him. "Mayhap you should have stayed home these last years to help your father, and he would not be in bed right now fighting for his life."

"Wait one minute." Danger glinted in his eyes. He strode forward, close enough for her to feel the heat of his breath and the bunched tension in his powerful body. "Are you accusing me—"

"I am saying that some people do not have a father. And they would have gladly stayed and worked a farm alongside him. Just to have him in her life." She blinked hard, biting her lip to keep from saying more. Did she have to let him see her heart?

Jonah only stared at her, his mouth open. A muscle jumped along his jaw. "You dare to judge me?"

"Why not? Some of us stayed." And at a greater cost. "Of course it is more difficult to impress hero-worshipping boys with homey little tales. No one calls a son who stays home a hero. Nor one who makes his ill father's life more comfortable."

"I did not leave home to make myself into a hero. No such animal exists." His hands fisted. Fury gleamed in eyes as dark as night. "I despise the word. Why do you keep saying I am one? Mayhap that is the way you see me?"

"Nay." But it was. Bigger than a man had a right to be, so handsome he could stop the moon from shining. Look at the way her hand still tingled where his fingers had touched her. Her heart thudded fast and hard at his nearness.

"You are the outsider here," he pointed out, "you and your unwanted opinions."

His anger glowed like an ember, changing his face, tangible like radiating heat.

An outsider. She felt as if he'd pared her with a knife and lay open her heart. Pain turned into anger, but she could only stare at him. What could she say? She'd lost the argument to this big, arrogant man who made her feel small and inadequate. Too short Too thin. Too plain. *Too disagreeable*.

That was the true reason no man had married her, despite her age, despite her circumstance. All those years fighting to keep a roof over her ill mother's head and enduring heartless relatives' scorn had forced a wall so thick around her heart even a marauding Indian could not breach it.

She never once truly resented caring for her mother, or missed too terribly the lost chances for fun other girls her age had enjoyed. But no, her life had not been easy. Maybe if she'd had more patience, or more faith, or more beauty . . .

But the truth was she'd become an outsider. The kind of woman only Horace Walling would marry.

Tessa ducked her chin and strode from the room.

"You were harsh with her."

Jonah rubbed his brow. His head throbbed with exhaustion; his heart ached with worry. "I know. She just made me angry. Probably because she was right."

"All I know is that she has been tending Father as if he were her own." Thomas paused to study the old man lying so still and the surgeon bleeding him with studious caution. "I don't see anyone else volunteering to stoke fires and change bedding and haul snow up a flight of stairs, then clean up the mess. Do you?"

"Not one of those young females hoping to marry me," Jonah added wryly.

Thomas' eyes crinkled, unable to manage a smile. "Mistress Tessa may be a man's worst nightmare, but I tell you, there is no one else I would rather have with Father right now. She's skilled, and she's got a gentle hand with the infirm."

"Too bad she doesn't have a gentle tongue to match." Jonah studied the tray Tessa had brought. Fresh biscuits and untouched corn pudding. She'd tended them, although no one had asked it of her. "I suppose I just like a woman who's biddable and pleasing."

"I could not agree with you more." Thomas reached for the teapot. "If you make her angry, she will leave. The surgeon says he can stay, but only as long as he can help."

"Aye." Wearily, Jonah sighed, so damn tired he couldn't focus his blurring eyes. "Mayhap I can repair the damage."

Hell, there was so much he couldn't repair. Like his father's illness. It killed him to think the old man was suffering so.

He left the room, his burden greater for having left the bedside. What if his father died while he was away? Jonah hesitated in the dark hallway, blending with the shadows.

A small sound, hardly more than a breath, but he heard it coming from the room farthest away. He strode through the dark, counting the doorways. The last stood ajar and inside he heard a delicate sniff, then silence.

"Tessa?" He gave the door a push.

"Go away." Anger edged her words.

He knew how easy it was to use anger to cover up deeper emotions, how easy to drive others away. "Nay, I have something to say and you have no choice but to listen."

" 'Tis a pity that you haven't changed in nearly twenty-five years, Hunter." A shadow shifted on the edge of the bed, a mere ribbon of shape. "You're still unbearably bossy. 'Tisn't as adorable on a thirty-year-old man."

"I never said I wanted to be adorable." He stepped into the room, blocking the threshold.

"Good thing. You'd fail miserably."

A smile stretched the corner of his mouth, despite the turmoil inside him. "I am sorry for how I treated you. For what I said."

"You are not." A tremble she couldn't hide in her voice. "You're just afraid if you make me too angry I'll refuse to stay and help with your father."

"That was Thomas' concern. He is a shallow, self-serving man. He was too cowardly to come himself."

A little choke. Ah, he'd nearly made her chuckle. "Shallow, self-serving traits run strong in the Hunter family, especially in the eldest son."

"Will you stay?" He had no time for humoring her, even if he genuinely regretted his words. Thoughtless, they were. Hell, he was so damn tired and scared that being angry with her had been easiest. He wasn't proud of himself, but at least he could admit it. And not make the mistake again.

"I would not walk away from anyone in so much need. Is that what you think of me?"

Not anger. Hurt. So, he was not the only one battling a reputation that did not fit. As he was no hero, she was no shrew. Not Tessa with her gentle hands. How many families had she helped over the years? How many had she nursed back from illness and injury? Or sat at a bedside easing the dying one's pain? And many of the good people of Baybrooke could only treat her with distance and shakes of the head?

"Nay. That is not what I think of you. Hell, you have done more for my own father than I have."

"True." He sensed a smile in that whisper-soft voice.

"Then you will accept my apology?" He reached for a match from the bureau. Struck it.

Light brushed over her face as he lit the taper.

"Nay. I would never accept your apology, Hunter. I would never know if it was sincere or not." She lifted her chin. Tears sheened her cheeks.

Jonah felt gut-punched. He had made her cry. He felt lower than dirt. What a clodpated dolt. "Tessa, I—"

"No pretenses." She stood, straightening her rumpled skirts. Candlelight brushed her body, highlighting the curves of her breasts. "You don't care about me. We both know that. Just walk away. Leave me alone. I will wash my face and have some tea and be in to change your father's bedding."

She dismissed him with a wave of her work-rough hand. Dismissed him. As if he were a mere private and she a general.

"I am not pretending, Tessa," he ground out. And then his gaze fell on the soft bow of her mouth.

Heat trembled through him along with the memory of her experienced kiss. Aye, it was enough to drown out the suffocating sadness in his heart.

"Well, neither am I, Hunter. My dislike of you is real."

But there was no venom in her words. A hint of softness, an invitation. "Do you dislike all men, or do you save that passion just for me?"

"I have no passion for you." She dipped her chin, and he could not see her face.

She sounded sad. Tiny tingles of want danced and tempted. He fought the urge to take her in his arms and hold her. Aye, how he remembered the feel of her against him. Heated softness. Willing woman. Even now his eyes appreciated the ample curves of her breasts, soft looking but firm. Heat licked through his blood.

"I meant what I said in there." She rubbed her hands together, red from manual labor so that they looked chapped even in this thin light. "You were lucky enough to have a kind man for a father. Yet you wasted the years you were given with him. What I would give—"

She stopped. He could not argue, could not deny her charge. No matter how angry he wanted to get, she was right. He sighed, fisting his hands. "I cannot change the past, Tessa. Is this what you want me to do?"

"No, I just—" She sniffed.

Hell, she was crying. Big tears that glimmered in the light, even though she bowed her face to hide them. He looked at his hands, so helpless. What did he do? He sensed her tears were genuine, a rare experience for him.

"You have a f-family," she whispered, her slender shoulders shaking within her too-large garment. "What I would give—"

Horace Walling. Jonah hadn't remembered her troubles. The world did not stop because his life was changing. He thought of Horace's rotten teeth and dirty hands. Jonah's stomach soured. "Hasn't your grandfather given you a different choice in a husband?"

"What other choice?" she whispered. "Grandfather has hated the burden I've been to his family. Where would I go? There are no other relatives left alive to take me."

She drew him in like a spell wrapped around his heart. Her voice, did it have to feel as if it touched his skin? The sweetness of it shifted over him like spun sugar. His groin tightened. Hell, what was his lusty body thinking? This was Tessa Bradford. And yet he could not stop wanting to lay her across the bed and bury his aching shaft inside her warm, willing body.

"Grandfather has forbidden me to work for hire." Her eyes shimmered, so wide and inviting. "I know 'Tis hard to believe of me, but I have dreams, too. And they do not include sharing a bed with Horace Walling."

Jonah took a step closer, breathless. Her eyes dazzled. Her mouth twisted into a vulnerable frown. An inviting frown that lured him.

Blood throbbed in his groin at the thought of Tessa Bradford naked in his bed.

"Will you tell anyone what I just said?" she asked now, avoiding his gaze as she looked to the stairway.

"Nay."

So, he affected her. Jonah liked the way she ducked her chin, keeping her face from his gaze. She wanted him, he guessed, with the same heated need as he felt for her. Honest and straightforward, the way it should be between a man and a woman. No emotions attached.

He thought of her midnight journey when he'd saved her from the wolves. Only a woman coming from a man's bed would be unescorted in the woods that time of night.

So, she was experienced. Perhaps that was what he needed. Guilt and remorse for the son he'd been threatened to drown him. And watching Father so close to death had been the hardest thing he'd done.

"I should get back to your father's side," she said with that sweet voice that could lure the devil.

"First, you must attend to me." He caught her chin in his hand, his groin heavy in anticipation. If he could bury this pain, it would go away. He felt certain of it. Jonah covered his mouth with hers.

He felt her surprise. At first her mouth was set against him, almost unresponsive. Almost. He closed his eyes, lost in the sweet, consuming fire. So greedy it pulsed through his veins like a storm of wind and flame, fast and intoxicating.

He curled a hand around her neck and tipped her head back to deepen the kiss. On a sigh, she melted into his arms. His blood kicked at the feel of her against him. The soft heat of her breasts seared his chest. The curve of her belly nudged his arousal. Want ripped through his veins. Damn, she was pure temptation, and she was beckoning him beyond all control.

"Your father," she gasped, breaking from his arms.

His breath came hard. Aroused and wanting, he simply stared at her and trembled from deep inside.

"Come quick!" Andy burst into the room.

In a heartbeat, Jonah spun away from Tessa, his need for comfort forgotten. "What is it?"

"Father is conscious," Andy choked.

"Thanks be, he is alive."

"Nay." Andy swallowed, tears spilling down his face. "The doctor says that often before a man dies he has a moment of clarity. Mayhap this is his. Father is asking for you, Jonah."

Nay. Every muscle in his body drew taut, and he could not move. *I cannot lose Father so soon. And not this way, not before I keep even this one vow.*

Yet he found his feet moving. Tessa forgotten, and Andy at his side. Then he was in Father's room and Thomas laid a hand on his shoulder. Well, he was not alone in his sorrow or his loss.

Together, they would face this. As brothers.

"Jonah." Father held out his hand at the first sound of a step inside the threshold.

If only he could hold back time, change the past, make himself into the man Father wanted. Jonah approached the bed, each step the hardest he'd ever taken.

"Father. I am here." He wrapped his hands tightly around the old man's, powerless to change fate, helpless against the consequences of his own long-ago decisions. "I never should have left you."

"You left home to make me proud," Father whispered, tears bright in his eyes. "And you do me proud now that you are home. Whatever happens, do not forget how very much I love my boys."

CHAPTER SIX

"'Tis morning, and still you haven't slept." Thomas strode into the room.

Jonah turned from the fire, the stick of wood in his hand, the fire popping and crackling. "And I will not sleep until the doctor says 'Tis over, either way."

Together, their gazes landed on the frail old man on the bed, washed and dry and swaddled with blankets, sleeping while Tessa stacked clean towels on the night table.

"There is naught we can do but wait," Thomas said. He meant to be comforting.

Jonah shrugged. Weariness rolled over him like an ocean wave. "I'm not so good at waiting."

"That makes two of us. Come and sample the cooking."

"Who's cooking?"

"Oh, the dozen or so marriageable females who all miraculously brought by breads and puddings and even cakes to help you in this time of difficulty." Thomas' eyes flashed with small humor. "A smart maiden never misses an opportunity to display her cooking talents to a prospective bridegroom."

"Don't remind me of my duty," Jonah growled, more tired than irritated. He took one long last look at Father, so lifeless, struggling so hard to hold on. "I should not leave him."

"Maybe he's expiring from the sight of that ugly face of yours, brother." Thomas' hand cupped his shoulder. "Come, have some coffee and eat. No doubt we'll all need our energy, either way it goes."

"I'll stay with him whilst you break your fast." Tessa looked up from her work changing the poultice on Father's chest. So dark those eyes, steady and deep. "I will call you if there is any change."

Thomas nodded, careful to keep his distance from her. "We're much obliged for all you've done, Mistress Tessa."

"You need not thank me." She turned, jaw set.

"You have run out of excuses, brother." Thomas' hand on the back of his shoulder guided him toward the door. "We will not be gone long, and 'twill give Father a respite from your dreadful presence."

"And yours, brother." Guilt and regret slowed Jonah's step as he followed his brother from the room. Aye, how his conscience troubled him. "I swore to marry before he died."

"What should you do?" Thomas answered ahead on the stairs. "Pick any girl and marry her the very day you return to town?"

"There lies my problem. I can't simply pick a girl. They look like children to me." His voice echoed in the empty and cold parlor as he followed his brother to the kitchen beyond. "I cannot marry a woman half my age."

"That's one of the difficulties of being thirty." Thomas grabbed a taper and lit it from the single candle burning in the table's center. "By that age, all the women are married or so ugly no one will have them."

"You're speaking of Tessa Bradford," he guessed. "Hell, what happened to this kitchen?"

"Women," Thomas muttered, shaking his head.

Women? The devil's teeth! It looked like a pack of bakers had descended on the house. "Father is dying. He doesn't need a final buffet."

"Final buffet. Last supper." Thomas shrugged. "Look, Andy has already helped himself. He's devoured half the cinnamon cake."

"I'm in deep trouble, brother, and you worry over missing pastry?" Jonah grabbed a cup and crossed the room. "I am to wed. I have little faith in marriage."

"Pray, don't say that too loudly. You are like to offend all the young ladies who made these treats and they will have you thrown in the stocks for a day." Thomas, even weary and grief-stricken, managed another joke.

"I cannot marry a mere girl." He gestured to the plate-laden table. Crocks, platters, rows of cakes and delicious treats crammed nearly every available inch. "They do not even know me. These efforts of theirs are far from sincere."

"You want sincerity? Then do not look for it in any woman." Thomas considered that. "Well, maybe a few women. But a damned few."

"Aye." Jonah knew they were both remembering their stepmother. "That woman made Father's life hell and took pleasure in it. I refuse to marry anyone even half as selfish."

"Or eager for your money." Thomas' telling gaze met his.

So, they shared the same worries. Jonah understood. "I have given my word. I must marry. There must be a son who will inherit this land."

"So, who will you choose?"

Jonah filled two cups with coffee, thinking. "If Father survives this illness, he will be infirm. Then I'll need a female willing to care for him as well as to manage the household. I shall not have a lazy wife sitting about, shouting at the servants."

"Our servants work the land and would not agree to clean house," Thomas added.

"True." Jonah set one cup before his brother and pulled a chair up to the board. "She must be kind. I don't want a cruel woman raising my son."

Again, he thought of his stepmother. Aye, the viciousness of that one. All of them bore scars in one way or another. Fear beat within his chest like a caged bird. What kind of woman could he tolerate for a wife?

"Most important, she must be a female I can see myself bedding, not a child half my age. If only we knew if Father was to recover for certain, I could take my time. Maybe travel to Boston and find someone appropriate."

"I don't envy you." Thomas sipped the steaming brew. "For once I'm glad I am not the eldest brother. Father is weak and we do not have much time."

"Aye. I do not need reminding." Jonah rubbed his face with both hands as if he could rub away the weariness, too. "I have been thinking a lot about the word. Duty. What it means. And what I must do."

"I have been pondering it as well." Thomas stepped away to choose a cheese tart from the offering on the table. His steps knelled heavily on the wood floor. "We all have left home following our own paths. Now, Father's illness has brought us back. To change. To carry on what he's worked hard for all his life."

"The land," Jonah sighed. "Family."

Aye, duty was a tough word. It required self-sacrifice, doing the right thing rather than making his own choices. And damn it, Jonah was a man used to forging his own path, facing challenges, and commanding men.

But that was a different duty, one that required only muscle and brain. It did not require heart.

"How will you choose your bride?" Thomas asked now.

"I have no idea, but I know this." Jonah remembered Father's face, pale and shrunken now that the frightening fever had broken. He was improving, but for how long? "I must make a decision."

"Today would not be fast enough." Thomas' hand landed on Jonah's shoulder.

His brother's understanding felt good, made him more brave. "How do I know the woman I select will make an unselfish wife and a kind mother, especially if I can't spend any time getting to know her?"

"There must be a way," Thomas murmured, sounding as perplexed as Jonah felt.

Duty. There was no denying, no stalling, and no excuses he could make. Now was the time to make good on his promise, to stand up and be the son his father wanted and needed. "Father is going to require constant care for some time, and the doctor fears he may never fully recover."

"Aye."

Jonah paused, considering. Inspiration struck. Why hadn't he thought of it before? "Then I'll need a wife willing to tend to Father. It would only be logical."

"Logical?"

A trickle of hope flickered inside Jonah's chest. Could it work? Why not? If he could find a woman who wouldn't mind caring for a sick old man, then perhaps . . .

The hope inside him grew, warming him from the inside out.

That would be the test, the way he would know which of those young, terribly inexperienced females had a genuinely caring heart. Maybe, just maybe, she wouldn't be the kind of female who would dominate his life or tear him apart with her guile.

"What are you saying, brother?"

"I think I've found a solution." Ah, it felt good to have at least one burden lifted. "This is a neighborly village. People care for one another, pitch in and help out when there is an illness such as Father's."

"What is your point?"

"I will watch the young women who come visit today." Jonah stood, his knees a little shaky, but his heart firmly resolved. "And I will marry the one who genuinely offers to do the most for Father."

"What? Have you gone mad?"

"Probably." Jonah could not deny it.

"What if it's the widow with the warts?" Thomas cried out, horrified.

Duty.

Jonah set his jaw. It mattered little what he wanted, only what he had to become.

The golden light of morning warmed the room with its cheerful presence, and Tessa knew she must leave. She had her furious grandfather to appease, who was only tolerating her long night of service to Colonel Hunter because Grandfather hoped to impress Jonah Hunter.

Violet was now of marriageable age, and apparently Grandfather had high hopes for her.

Half stumbling, Tessa carried the sheets to the kitchen and piled them by the back door. Surely one of the Hunters' servants would know to wash the sheets. As it was, she was far too weary to do more than find her way home.

Of course, more work awaited her there.

"Are you leaving?"

Jonah's rich voice warmed her like rum. Such reactions she had to this man. Tessa lifted her chin. "Chores are awaiting me at home."

"I understand. I don't know how to thank you for all you've done for my father." Jonah smiled, tired and troubled, but that smile stretched all the way to his eyes.

Such deep eyes, a woman could get lost inside them. Lose all common sense. She knew the taste of his passionate kisses, knew the heady luxury of being enfolded in his strong arms. 'Twas a feeling she had only dreamed of before now.

Then she shook her head, dispersing the spell he cast on her. The way he was looking at her, and remembering the liberties she'd allowed him, made her blush. "I help anyone who's ill. Coming here was nothing out of the ordinary."

"Oh." The light died in his spectacular eyes.

Tessa's heart darkened at the sight. She didn't want Jonah to think she was doing him any special favors. Still, she hadn't meant to hurt him. He'd been absent from this village a long time, didn't realize she helped wherever she could. Knowing Jonah, he probably thought she'd come especially because of him, the self-important oaf.

Now at least he no longer thought so, even if he didn't gaze at her with eyes of liquid heat.

"When your father awakens, give him a cup of the tea I left right there." She gestured. "By the hearth."

He was a man of silence, of unreadable emotion sheltered in the shadows. Solid and strong as steel. The sight of him made her heart catch.

He cleared his throat, his voice as somber as a funeral. "Thank you, Tessa. You are a better woman than most"

Dark eyes snared hers, cool but somehow intimate.

"You're very pretty when you smile. You should do it more often."

"False flattery doesn't fool me."

"Then I shall have to try all the harder."

Captivating. He could lure the angels from heaven with that slow stretch of a grin. It was lopsided and carved a dimple into his left cheek.

"I thought charm comes naturally to a man like you."

"Aye, 'Tis a gift" His smile deepened, lighting his eyes.

Touching her heart.

Tessa's head reeled. Air wedged in her lungs. "You best watch out for lightning after telling a lie like that"

"So, now I'm a liar." Two dimples shaped his smile, so wickedly handsome her brain forgot to function.

"A charming liar. A lethal combination." Tessa swallowed. What was she doing, bantering with this man? What would her grandfather say if he knew? Pain twisted in her heart *No one will ever want to marry a sharp-tongued spinster like you. You are ugly, skinny and disagreeable. You ought to be grateful Horace Walling agreed to take you, but I had to throw in a cow with the deal.*

Those words rang like a death knell in her head, so sharp and clear from the morning when she'd returned from the Hunters' house, her grandfather holding the ruined cloak up as evidence.

There would be no loving marriage, no happy home for her. And what of the child she wanted so badly? How could she let Horace . . . Lord, she could not even stomach the thought. There was no way she would beget a child without love. Duty wasn't good enough. Not for her heart. And not for the daughter of her dreams.

"I'll try to return some time after noon, if I can get away from my work." Tessa lifted her shawl from the wall peg.

"Not if, when." Jonah stepped into the thin light Fire flickered in his eyes. "If Father takes a bad turn, then I will come to fetch you. Whether your grandfather can spare you or not."

His command whirled her around, temper stirring. "And consequences be damned, right?" Tessa raged. "Why would you care? 'Tis not your life and not your hide if Ely becomes angry."

"I care only about my father." A muscle jumped in his tightly clenched jaw, square and hard. There were no dimples, only furious power and muscle-hard man. If softness lived within him, she could not see it now.

What had she expected? Jonah was nothing more than the very type of man she feared. Pushy. Domineering. Never saw himself as wrong. "This is not the militia, Hunter. You are not a commander, and I will not be ordered by you."

"What? Now you're refusing to come help my father?" Jonah roared, fury snapping through him like lightning.

"I will come." She wanted to give him a good thwack with her basket. Knock some civility into him. "But don't think that I am helping your father because you asked me."

"Not even in my wildest dreams."

Anger emanated from him like heat from a hearth. Tensed his strong jaw. Drew taut his magnificent shoulders.

His words struck her like a blow. No man would dream of her.

Oh, she knew why he'd sought her out for a kiss. He was afraid and wanted comfort, that was all.

She didn't want to be reminded of it. She clenched her teeth, willing her hurt to stay buried deep in her heart, and headed straight for the door, her basket clutched in both hands.

She would not look back. She would not let him see how accurate his aim had been. A blow straight to the heart, like only a man could do. Even Jonah Hunter, so revered and heroic everyone in the village respected him. Then how would Horace Walling treat her? How could she begin to expect anything but servitude from her inconveniently arranged marriage?

Damn Jonah Hunter. That was his fault, too. If he hadn't blackmailed her, Grandfather never would have decided to rid her from his house for good.

Tessa faced the grayness of morning and started the long journey home.

"If you make her angry, she might not come back," Thomas pointed out reasonably. "And you know well, brother. We need her help."

"No longer than it takes for me to find a wife, then Tessa Bradford will never darken my doorstep again." Jonah chugged down a long pull of cooled coffee. He felt bad for her and he appreciated her knowledge and help, but that didn't mean he liked her.

"Never say never, brother. That always leads to trouble." Thomas emptied his cup. "Father is holding his own."

"He drank two cups of that tea." Jonah's heart warmed simply remembering. Father had been weak, but managed a smile. And commented how Tessa's tea tasted as bad as bird droppings.

"And 'Tis still morning. Nearly eleven o'clock."

Thomas managed a lopsided grin. " 'Tis a wonder only a dozen women have paid a call, clamoring for a piece of you."

"Please, don't remind me. 'Twas terrifying." He immediately thought of his stepmother and the way she'd treated their father, all of them, draining the joy from every day and happiness from every aspect of life. Would this be his married fate?

"Will they bring more food, I wonder?" Andy bolted in the back door from the barn. "Since we lost cook we've had to get along on Thomas' cooking skills."

"When more women arrive, they will certainly bring more food." Jonah faced the window. Light filtered through low clouds. He would choose his wife today.

If she were kind, then she would be good enough.

A knock rattled through the silent house.

"Mayhap that is your future wife," Thomas teased with a wink. "Well, there's only one way to know for certain. Get on your feet and answer the door, man."

"I hope it isn't the widow with the warts," Andy mused. "I've tasted her biscuits at the husking bee last autumn. Terribly dry. 'Tis better to pick a wife who's a good cook, too."

Jonah gritted his teeth and stood to face his destiny.

"Tell me what the house is like," Violet demanded, her ardor not diminished by the splash of sudsy wash water.

"Just a house, 'Tis all. Bigger than this one." Tessa rinsed the bowl and set it on the toweled table to dry.

"You're lying because you just don't want me to know. I bet the Hunters' parlor is a fine one. I've seen the huge windows and the clapboards so neat and cared for. Inside the parlor must be huge, with velvet everywhere."

"I was too busy to notice whether the chair was velvet or not" Tessa plunged her hands into the sink. The last man she wanted to talk about was Jonah Hunter.

"I bet there are glass lamps everywhere, with the candles inside. And crystal teardrops catching the light." Violet swelled up with great hope.

"I saw only candleholders, plain as glass. I was tending an ill man, not drooling over his material possessions." Tessa scrubbed hard at the iron kettle. Berry sauce darkened the wash water.

"I don't care about the old colonel. 'Tis Major Hunter I have an eye on."

"Just like every girl in the entire village." Tessa rinsed and set the kettle to dry. Exhaustion fogged her brain, yet she lifted a clean towel from the pile and began drying the dishes, the third set today.

"Do you think the pink ribbon's best?" Violet held up both a blue and a pink ribbon against her dress.

"I doubt Jonah Hunter is a man to notice a foolish girl's ribbons." She wasn't jealous, she was damn mad. After a long night of work with hardly any sleep, she'd done nothing but do her chores here. The barn, the meals, the dishes, care of the milk, the daily sweeping, and then making a batch of berry tarts for the silly chit to take to the Hunters' house.

To pay a call, as Charity said. But Tessa knew the truth. They wanted to show off Violet to Hunter and make him notice her youthful beauty and thoughtfulness in the gift of tarts.

What the colonel's illness had to do with pastry, Tessa did not understand. The old man needed clean sheets and a hearty soup broth he could sip and special tea to boost his recovery.

The berry tarts were for Jonah.

A knock rattled on the door, startling her. A knife slipped from her hands to the floor.

"Clumsy," Violet scolded.

Tessa tossed the dishtowel on the table. "Oh, go bat your eyes at Jonah Hunter. You ought to be perfect for him. You both are so in love with yourselves, neither of you could love anyone else."

"Why you low-down, dried-up—"

A baby's cry shrilled through the room.

Violet paled.

Tessa turned, dread filling her heart. Horace Walling stood in the doorway, holding an outstretched basket in one arm and an infant in the other.

His rotten teeth flashed when he talked. "Your grandfather said you would see to some of the daily work. I brought by the family's clothes for you to wash. Guess you might as well get accustomed to it. By this time next week, it'll be your lot in life."

Tessa took one look at Charity's and Violet's triumphant smiles and bit her lip.

There is no way on this green earth, she wanted to say but held her tongue. Temper stirred in her chest, and she fought it.

Be his wife? *Not on her life.*

* * *

"A lovely caller to see you, Jonah," Andy yodeled from the base of the stairs.

Jonah turned from the fire in his father's room, the stick of wood in hand. "Another caller?" he muttered wearily to his other brother.

Thomas stood from the low bedside stool, studied the slumbering face of the man lying there, and stretched. "At least we will not be in danger of starving."

"Aye. I have never seen so many breads, stews, soups and puddings gathered together in my life." Weariness rolled over him like an ocean wave. "So many visitors and not one offer to help with Father. All the young ladies have offered calculated smiles, their plates of food, and sometimes a shy offer of something else."

It was that something else that soured his stomach.

Thomas fidgeted on the chair. "I see how you worry. 'Tis fearsome, after growing up watching our stepmother use Father."

"Aye." It saddened him to think he could be in the same position.

"Father couldn't see that our stepmother did not want love and passion, but to live in his fine house and drain dry the coffers buying enough silk dresses to clothe every living subject in all of the colonies."

"I'll not make the same mistake." Jonah rubbed his brow. "And it makes me afraid to see what manner of female will greet me next at the door."

"Be brave, brother. Andy and I will protect you from any forward virgins." Humor sparkled in Thomas' dark eyes.

"Fie, you are a scoundrel to tease me." Jonah strode from the room, listening to his brother's laughter.

He was a fool for making such a vow, this promise of marriage. It seemed his faith in females fell even lower today. 'Twas nearly suppertime and not one of his fourteen visitors had offered to help him tend Father.

What would he do then?

Voices rumbled, growing clearer as he approached. He strode into the lit parlor, and his gaze froze on the two female forms huddling before the fire. One was dressed in pink and blue, dressed and groomed and smiling so hugely. Far too young for his taste.

The other female was skinny. Black curls tumbled over the back of her tattered shawl. Simple blue homespun skirts rustled as she turned from the hearth to face him.

Tessa Bradford had come to call on him?

"Jonah. Did you brew the tea I left for your father?" Her voice held a low bite.

But he remembered the softness in her eyes, the vulnerability. And the gentleness he'd witnessed behind the terrifying spinster mask.

"Father hated the tea and told me next time you were to leave something more palatable or he would come after you himself."

"Tell the stubborn old man he's no match for me." A sweetness warmed her eyes, even if the tight line of her mouth did not ease. "I'll head upstairs and check on him."

So, she hadn't come to call, but to keep her promise. Why his gaze followed her through the parlor, he couldn't begin to speculate. She was a completely disagreeable female, but his blood thickened simply watching her. He remembered her hot kisses and an unspoken promise of seductive passion, and his breeches grew tighter.

He wondered about her lover, the man she'd been meeting on the night he fired on the wolves. Was she passionate and wild with him? Jonah could see it, could sense beneath the unbending primness that Tessa Bradford could drive a man beyond all control.

"Major Hunter?" a low voice rose and fell over his name like a caress.

He snapped his head around. Plump and pretty Violet Bradford looked up at him through her lashes.

"I baked berry tarts just for you." She held out the wooden platter, probably the best the family owned, and dipped her chin.

He did not miss the shine in her eyes when her gaze swept the room.

"You baked these tarts?" He took the cloth-covered plate. Disappointment, nay, it was worse than disappointment, flooded his chest. "From what I hear Tessa does all the domestic tasks."

"She lies. I'm quite capable—"

"She had to leave my father's side this morning to prepare breakfast for your family," he ground out, illogically furious. "That is a daughter's duty. Aren't you the eldest daughter?"

"Aye, but—"

"So tell me," he demanded, "even if you did bake these tarts yourself, which I doubt, then why were you making foolish sweets to impress me when you should have been preparing the meals so Tessa could tend my seriously ill father?"

Violet's seductive mouth crumpled and tears filled her eyes. She flew from the room.

"You were harsh with her," Andy observed from the kitchen doorway.

"Aye, I regret it." Confusion tore at him. He stared down at the plate. "I don't know what came over me."

"I distinctly heard berry tarts mentioned." Andy bounded into the room. "Here, let me take that terrible burden from you. A man contemplating marriage has no use for berry tarts."

"And I suppose a man not contemplating marriage does?"

"Aye, a serious need." Andy peeked beneath the cloth. "Hmm. These smell heavenly."

"Thank you." Tessa breezed into the room, dark curls falling into her eyes as she managed a small smile. "I hope you like them, even if you probably have an entire kitchen of baked goods by now."

His heart knocked hard against his ribs. Jonah took a step back. "You take my brother's compliment, but not mine."

A small smile twinkled in eyes as dark as night. "That's because your brother is not an overbearing oaf."

Andy chuckled. "True. Thank you for the tarts, Mistress Tessa. These are the best we've received today. I'm off to devour them."

Jonah waited until his brother had left the room. His throat dried. He lifted his gaze and saw her face, half hidden by a few thick untamed curls falling from her muslin cap. "Whilst Father is improved from last night, he is still so weak and frail. Do you think he will live?"

"I wish I could say for sure." Tessa hugged the ends of her shawl tight around her, drawing the knit wool to cloak her well-shaped breasts.

Fire sparked through his veins, making it damn hard to think. "His fever has broken."

"A good sign, but his lungs are greatly affected. Your father is still gravely ill." She dipped her chin, and he could not read her face. As if she were suddenly shy, she took a step toward the door, then hesitated. "I know you can afford to bring in help and you may not want my services, especially after the way I lost my temper this morning."

"I hardly noticed."

She took another step toward the door. "I have a terrible flaw in my temper, I know, but until your father is stronger and if you want me to help out, I wouldn't mind."

Silence filled the house, as if her softly spoken, amazingly quiet words had been blasted from a mountaintop.

Jonah's heartbeat stuttered. "Wh-what did you say?"

"I know the indentured servant Sarah left last month after fulfilling her contract with your father, and you've no female help to care for him." Tessa looked longingly at the door, as if she'd rather be anywhere but standing before him. "I'm usually asked to help in times like these, but I already understand why you might not want me here. I just can't abide the thought of a dear old man so ill without wanting to help."

"I have to sit down." Jonah's knees buckled, and he eased onto a nearby footstool. "You like my father?"

"He was kind enough to help me when I needed it once, when not even family would." Tessa's eyes filled with tears, amazing tears that shimmered like silver in her eyes, then spilled down her creamy cheeks.

Honest, genuine tears that reminded Jonah of the woman who'd turned down the fine wool cloak when she needed one.

"Long ago, my mother required a doctor, but there was no money for one. The colonel sent one and paid the fees. I hadn't even spoken of it to anyone but the minister. Yet your father brought out a fine doctor all the way from Boston, and it truly made a difference in easing my mother's suffering."

Jonah remembered Tessa's ill mother, a thin woman so pale and weakened by a palsy and other afflictions that she couldn't walk.

Tessa swiped at her cheeks, drying her tears. "It would mean much to me to care for your father now, to repay him in this small way. I need to do this. If you will let me."

Andy cleared his throat from the kitchen threshold. "She bakes a perfect berry tart, Jonah. Aye, a fine cook indeed."

His heart stopped beating for an entire minute. Jonah saw Thomas' shadow in the stairwell and knew he'd heard Tessa's plea.

His entire body quaked, but he managed to stand. Reached out and took Tessa's small, work-reddened hand. "I would be honored if you would help us."

A small smile warmed her face and lit up her eyes like a morning sun. He saw the goodness within, a genuine happiness that he'd accepted her offer.

"I think I'll go upstairs right away and see what the colonel needs. Thank you, Jonah. You have allowed me to repay a long-standing debt, and it means more to me than you know."

She spun away, darting up the stairs with a grace that bewitched him. Fire licked through his groin, filled his chest with longing.

And dread.

Andy's laughter filled the silent room. "I bet you ten pounds she'll refuse to marry you. She hates you, Jonah."

He rubbed his brow, confused, enamored, horrified. "Aye. I don't think I have ever been this terrified in my life."

CHAPTER SEVEN

"Andy is scared of you," the old colonel croaked, his voice nothing more than a whisper.

"I did my best." Tessa smoothed the clean sheet across Samuel Hunter's chest. "I'm glad to see I was successful."

The old man gasped for air, choking on a laugh. "That a girl. Don't give 'em an inch. Andy said you handled Jonah with the confidence of a general."

"He exaggerates." Tessa wrung excess from the washcloth, water splashing and tinkling in the china basin. "Lie back or you're going to start coughing."

"Nonsense," the old man croaked, then coughed.

Tessa set down the cloth and reached for the water pitcher. "I told you so."

A smile lit Samuel's eyes as he continued to cough. A shallow, painful rasp that worried Tessa. She poured a cup of cool water and held it to his lips.

"What did you do to deserve such royal treatment, old man?" Jonah strode into the room, wide shouldered and all male power.

A tiny flame burst to life in Tessa's chest. She ducked her chin and grabbed the cloth to dry Samuel's chin.

"Son, I'm on death's door, that ought to account for something." He gasped for air. "Give me more of that water, Tessa."

She liked the tough old bird. She held the cup steady as he struggled to drink. Heat burned across the bridge of her nose, then in a straight line down to her mouth. 'Twas Jonah's gaze, as tangible as fire. She looked up. His elemental gaze held her tight as a snare.

Like a trapped rabbit, her heart thudded. Her knees knocked. She glanced at the door and considered how on earth to escape.

"I need to speak to Tessa." Jonah's voice rumbled like a caress, stroking over her skin with heat and promise.

Danger. She could not allow this to go any further, this senseless physical longing for a man who was . . . was *indecent*. He was overbearing, bossy, and arrogant. What was attractive about that?

Apparently a lot. Her blood roared like liquid fire through her veins.

"You need to speak to me, eh? Well, I don't want to listen." That's right, scare him off, too. It worked with young Andy Hunter and the rest of the village.

"Oh, I think you will want to hear what I have to say."

"Do not be so certain."

Big fingers curled around her wrist

Tiny explosions pulsed up her arm.

"You two go talk," Samuel wheezed. "Let a poor old man sleep."

Tessa wasn't fooled by the small smile curving his mouth. She set down the cup and stood, her gaze fastening on the one man who could sneak past her defenses. "Fine. Then we will talk out in the hall, where I can be handy in case your father needs anything."

Jonah's eyes darkened with protest.

"Go on. I don't need a thing and besides, I can tell that you two want to be alone." The old man waved one hand.

"Come, let's go for a walk."

Lord, he was an enormous man, all brawny shoulders and powerful arms and a chest as broad as a woman's dreams. Tessa swallowed.

"A walk?" She couldn't imagine where they might walk.

" 'Tis pleasant in the sunshine." He gestured toward the small window.

"Surely, in nearly freezing weather."

"I'll lend you a cloak." Smooth as rum, sly as a devil, Jonah drew her around the bed, his grip on her wrist as firm as a manacle. Grim determination shone in his eyes. How he looked so exhausted. Tiny lines fanned out from the corners of his eyes. Darkness bruised the tanned skin beneath. Even the skin beneath the high cut of his cheekbones looked hollow.

She hadn't realized. He needed to discuss matters concerning his father's health. Of course that could not be spoken within the patient's hearing.

"I'm finished here for now," she managed in a light voice, determined to do her duty by Samuel Hunter. "I'll meet you outside, Jonah."

His dark eyes flashed a warning. What was he feeling? She couldn't tell. Not with the grim set of his square jaw, his lips a tightly compressed line. A prickle of foreboding wrapped around her chest.

* * *

What was taking Tessa so damn long? Jonah paced in the backyard, the fallow garden nothing but a row of humps beneath the half-frozen layers of snow, ice and mud.

He could picture her gathering up the wet towels and carrying them with the basin to the kitchen. Tessa, so neat and thorough, was also taking too damn much time. He wanted to get this over with.

He wasn't at all sure he could find the courage to do it.

Marry her? How his brothers had howled, bending double with the irony of it all. Yet it all came down to duty. Who else would tend her father? All but for her heart-tender feelings for the old man, she was completely unsuitable. Everything about her was wrong. From her sparse skinniness to her outrageously bossy ways.

A man wanted a biddable wife, someone he could lead. Make decisions for. Be in charge of. A man's place was at the head of the family, not being browbeaten by a woman twice as smart as he.

"I wager five pounds he falters," Thomas had challenged Andy's bet not an hour before. Serious minded Thomas. Who frowned upon wagers of any sort.

He could always back out. That was it. Jonah studied the wrapped parcel in his hands. Hell, he didn't have to marry her. The mere thought of it . . .

And yet she did not covet his wealth. They were close in age. And there was a tenderness in her touch when she tended her father. Such a thing could not be faked.

Aye, but life with her would be . . .

"Jonah?" She crossed the porch with a light step, facing into the wind. The current lifted back the tangle of untamed curls from her forehead and brushed her loose clothes back against her body.

She was a slight thing, fine boned and deceptively delicate. Her blue gaze speared his, and his mouth opened but nothing came out.

Run for your life, man.

"I know the doctor fears your father mightn't recover." She lifted her skirts above the frozen ground and soft patches of mud. "This must be a hard time for you."

His gaze landed on her slim fingers clutching that simple fabric. He knew damn well she'd helped grow the flax and harvest it, spun the thread and woven it, cut and sewed the skirts herself. One look at her callused hands told him she'd never had a respite in her life, never had it easy, and would never be a lazy, self-indulgent person.

Just what he was looking for in a wife. Except she was Tessa Bradford.

"Aye. The doctor is not certain, but he has reason to fear the worst." Jonah tore his gaze from hers. Agitated, he started pacing. What the hell was he going to do?

Andy and Thomas were probably in one of the rooms behind him, sneaking glances between the curtains through the window. He could not see them but felt the amused weight of their gazes.

"I hope you didn't come out here to try to kiss me again." Her chin came up, and she looked ready to fight.

Jonah figured she needed to be tough just to survive in Ely's household. Maybe if she weren't so overworked and ill treated, she would be more biddable. Maybe. He wasn't sure.

"Because if you want another kiss, I—"

"Marry me." He blurted the words because he couldn't figure out another way to say them.

Her bow shaped mouth fell open. "What did you say?"

Oh, Lord, what had he done? He'd proposed to her. Just like that. This was wrong, wrong, wrong. What would life be like married to strong willed Tessa?

But the image of her tending Father, her gentle hands soothing cool water across his brow, assured him. She was the right one.

Besides, she'd worked harder making soups and teas and gruel for Father, changing his sheets, washing him, fearing over his fever, and going without sleep than all the women combined with their breads and puddings and pastries.

Duty. He repeated the word until he felt fortified.

Tears shimmered in her eyes. He realized she'd been staring at him silent for an entire minute. Silent. Perhaps he was right. Perhaps the problem with Tessa Bradford was that she was unhappy and overworked. Maybe it wouldn't be so bad after all.

Even if he felt damn awkward, he held out the package. The cloak he offered her earlier. "I want you to have this."

Her lower lip trembled. "Why are you teasing me like this?"

"What?" Jonah shook his head. Something wasn't working properly in his brain. He thought she'd said—"Teasing you?"

Her soft face crumpled, and she looked so heartbroken he had no idea what to do—or what he'd done.

"You." Tears spilled down her cheeks. "You think this is funny? That you can play a joke like this?"

She thought this was a joke? "Tessa, I—"

"You are a heartless, cruel cad, Jonah Hunter, and I will hate you to the end of my days." She swiped at those tears, but they came faster now. "You know darn well what my fate is. Do you think I want to marry Horace? Don't you think I'm terrified? How dare you—"

A sob wracked her slim body, shaking her like a young tree in the wind.

Jonah stared down at the carefully wrapped cloak, uncertain what he'd done to make her think— Where was she going?

He looked up to see the flap of her skirts and the stiff set of her narrow back. Anger punctuated her fast steps, and he could tell she was still swiping at her tears.

Jonah took off after her, dashing across uneven ground. "Tessa. Wait a minute."

She broke into a run.

Damn, she was fast, too. He raced after her. Cold air beat at his face. Confusion pulsed through him. He only knew he'd hurt her. She thought he'd been teasing her.

"Tessa." His free hand closed around her elbow.

"Leave me alone. You've had your fun." A sob twisted her last word, leaving him feeling big and foolish and helpless.

Damn, just what he didn't expect from her.

"Tessa." He pulled her to a stop, swung her around to face him.

"Listen to me."

Tears silvered her eyes. Her lower lip quivered. Another sob broke through her.

"Tessa, I'm sorry." Damn it, he didn't know what to do. He was used to working with soldiers, and they sure as hell didn't cry. She looked vulnerable, felt so small. His entire hand fit easily around her elbow.

"I shall never forgive you." Another wobbly sob.

Contrite. Confused. Hell, he wasn't handling this the right way. "Tessa, I hope—"

He stopped. She was crying and he didn't know what to do, how to make her stop. Tears kept spilling down her face, one after another, silent and sorrowful.

It was so simple to reach out and brush at those tears with his fingertips. More tears came, but this time her gaze met his, so full of hurt he didn't know what to say.

Propose to her. Remember your duty. Father. Procreation.

At least he liked the prospect of procreating with her. His groin ached at the thought of her in his bed, those dark tangles of curls fanning across his pillow and clutched in his hands as she surrendered her body to him.

"I want to marry you."

She blinked, spilling more tears. "You d-don't." She sniffed, and even that seemed vulnerable. "Stop saying that"

She didn't believe him. Confused, he stared down at her, his heart pounding like Indian war drums. At least he knew she didn't covet his possessions, didn't want him for his money. 'Twas a good start.

"Tessa." He released his hold on her and began unwrapping the bundle he carried. The thinning daylight revealed the length of fine folded wool.

"I have to go," she whispered. "I have supper to prepare for Grandfather's family."

"Don't go." He meant it as an order, but it came out like a request. He shook out the cloak.

She drew in a shaky breath. "I'll be back to tend your father. I shouldn't be gone more than two hours."

She wasn't ever going to slave for that ungrateful family again. Jonah laid the cloak across her thin shoulders, so close he could smell the faint scent of wild roses in her hair. His guts clenched.

Blood drummed through unmentionable parts of his body.

"You said a cloak this fine should go to my wife, the wife I've come home to marry." She deserved a little kindness. He'd hurt her feelings. Had he been so thoughtless to her? Shame filled him. He'd proposed, and she was so unsure of him she mistakenly believed he would hurt her cruelly. Now, what did she believe?

"I can't be your wife, Jonah." Another sniff. More tears vibrating in her eyes, so dark and drawing he could not look away.

"Forget Horace Walling. You will not be marrying him." "

When he expected a smile, maybe a thank you and her undying gratitude for saving her from such a fate, Tessa shrugged off the cloak. Her slim fingers held the garment as if it were made of pure gold.

Her chin went up. Her entire body stiffened. "Why would you want to marry me?"

"Well, I—" *Duty.* He stopped before the explanation passed his lips. He didn't need to explain. She'd lived a lifetime of duty caring for her mother and earning her keep with relatives who didn't want her. He knew without asking she would care for his father with the same sense of duty.

Besides, she was wise enough to know, unlike those foolish young girls, that marriage was an agreement. A contract. A simple physical coexistence.

Her gaze studied him with pointed intelligence, searching his eyes and his face. Then her face changed. A light warmed her eyes, unlike anything he'd ever seen. A sweetness that drew him, made him feel as if he'd done the right thing after all.

"You really want to marry me."

So, she finally understood. Jonah's heart warmed. He reached out and took the cloak from her hands. Without a word, he held it out and she slipped into it, the fine wool curling over her shoulders as if she were made for it.

"What you're saying is that you love me." A question wrinkled her brow, but the brightness in her eyes doubled. A warmth just for him that held him spellbound.

"Love you?" he repeated.

Another tear rolled down her cheek. "Jonah, I never thought"

He didn't want to deceive her. He didn't want to use her. Jonah rubbed his brow, uncertain what to do next. How did he explain he would never love a woman, never give over the control of his heart the way his father had?

"I swore to myself long ago," she began, head down, shimmering black curls hiding her face, "when my mother suffered so married to my stepfather, that if it were in my power, I would only marry for love."

Love. There was that word again. That empty word that meant a person thought they could use you. Romantic love was about power and control. And love was little different than the battlefield, casualties and fighting and all.

Jonah didn't want love. He wanted peaceable coexistence.

He opened his mouth, but he knew any explanation would bring back those tears of hurt. He could not do that to her, no matter his personal opinion of Tessa Bradford, because she cared so much for his father.

She lifted her face and he could see all the hope in those eyes and all the uncertainty. Her voice sounded brave when she whispered, "I want to marry you."

CHAPTER EIGHT

He'd made a mistake. A terrible, horrible mistake. Jonah gazed down into dreamy blue eyes, as clear as dreams, and saw how wrong he'd been. He should have guessed that the woman who had tended Father with gentle hands and an angel's light was the same woman who instilled fear in the strongest men in this village with her sharp bold tongue.

Beneath the determined shell lived a tender heart. He had assumed a spinster who had seen as much of life and death as Tessa had would see his proposal as the practical arrangement he'd intended.

But how tremulous she looked, as if she could melt against his chest in disbelief.

Guilt speared him. Hero, they called him. Major, a leader of men. Hell, he gazed down at Tessa Bradford, saw a rare beauty brushing her face with the same luminous light as the pale sun, and turned coward. Full-fledged, yellow-bellied coward.

He knew he should tell her the truth. But how could he? She looked amazing, like the first blushing light of dawn. Crisp breezes ruffled her ebony curls and painted her cheeks pink. He could not take his gaze from the sight of her beauty so rare; he'd never seen the like before.

Then the light so blue in her eyes dimmed, the joy ebbed from her face until there was no light, no beauty. Only the plain face of duty and hardship. "I want to marry you, but I cannot. I am already promised. Money and livestock have changed hands and it can't be undone. Besides, there is no way Grandfather would ever let me—"

She held out the cloak to him, regret so dark on her face 'twas as if something precious inside her had died. "I'm sorry I got carried away. I just thought—I mean, I would have liked to marry you. Even if—"

"Even if you hate me?"

She blushed. And he saw the truth then. She didn't hate him. The taste of her kiss, heated velvet and passion, the feel of her slim woman's body held tight against him, the silken luxury of her curls, and the music of her voice came to him, memories that would haunt him this night and for many to come. She was an enchantress beneath her hard spinster image, one that she wore like a cloak to disguise the woman beneath.

He was no longer fooled. She was no child half his age, no whimpering female full of wiles and manipulations. Her hands, rough from harsh lye soap and chapped from the cold winter temperatures, testified she was a woman who knew how to work and did so willingly. And she loved his father.

He could think of no greater gift to the man he loved above all, the man he owed his life and his loyalty and all that he was.

"Keep the cloak, Tessa."

" 'Twould not be right. Others will say—"

"I don't give a damn what others say. All that matters is that it is cold outside and you have no serviceable cloak. It would make me happy knowing you wore it, someone who values my father so. Besides, he would want you to have it."

Were those more tears glimmering like rare diamonds in her eyes? " 'Tis too fine for me to wear. I will save it as a treasure."

She bowed her chin and simply walked away, her shadow slim and elongated from the low slant of the sun. Birds pecking for their sustenance upon the frosted ground scattered at her approach.

"Tessa."

She stopped, then turned. "What is it now?"

He stood squinting into the brightness, one hand at his brow to shield his eyes. Even simply dressed in black trousers and a dark tailored shirt, with the collar open to expose the strong column of his neck, he looked every bit the heroic major, a commander of men, brave and loyal.

He had proposed to her. To her, Tessa Bradford. His fine house towered behind him, two stories of well-constructed clapboard and a dozen diamond paned windows that winked and gleamed at the touch of the day's lemony light. It was hard to admit, but 'twas all too fine for her. If Grandfather knew, if Violet or her step-grandmother knew, how they would laugh at her.

"Let me take you home." He strode toward her, mighty and powerful. " 'Tis the least I can do for keeping you from your chores again."

" 'Tis a long walk," she conceded, daring to take a step toward him.

"What? Can it be that the feared spinster is being agreeable for once?" Humor glinted in his coffee dark eyes.

"I shall only be agreeable to you, and only this once." She took another step, and it was easier accepting his offer of help, of kindness. She had grown never to trust such gestures, for she had learned the hard way that she could never trust a man's motives. "Grandfather is likely to be angry that I'm so late."

"I will speak with him. Mayhap I can convince him out of his anger."

Gratefulness shone in her eyes. She had worked so hard tending his father, and the reason the frail old man now lived was in great part due to her quiet, tender, and knowledgeable care.

As Jonah led the way to the stable, he did not know what to say. Now that he'd made his mind up, he thought Tessa adequate for his wife. Nay, not just adequate, but the best choice he could make.

He hitched up the mare, a fine bay, one of Father's favorites, then offered his arm. But she climbed up onto the high seat herself, the cloak still folded around her shoulders, her chin down, her face unreadable.

"My brother Andy likes your berry tarts," he said, to break the silence as he took the reins. "He might eat like a horse, but he has a discerning palate."

She blushed with pleasure. "I noticed you did not sample my pastries."

"I had little appetite. If I had eaten anything, it would have been your tarts. 'Tis the frosting, I think, that makes them appealing."

"The frosting is a family secret from my mother's side." She almost smiled as the wagon rocked over the rutted patches in the road. "I believe I'm the only living soul who still knows the recipe."

The wind caressed loose dark tendrils across her alabaster brow, touching the satin softness of her face. Jonah well remembered the soft lustrous feel of her skin, and blood heated his veins, warming him despite the cool temperatures. "I didn't know my father went to dame school with your mother."

"Neither did I. Not until she was gravely ill and Grandfather refused to let us stay in his home any longer."

"What happened then?"

Shadows from a tall grove of trees blocked the light and cast her in shadow. "The colonel came and convinced my uncle to take us for a time. I shall never forget how he simply appeared at the door one day, even though neither my mother nor I summoned him. He made our lives better. His servant came with a cart to carry our few possessions and Mother, since she was not strong enough to walk."

"And he provided a doctor."

"A fine surgeon from Boston who stayed for three weeks, until he could do no more." Sadness swept across her face like the shadows of the trees, translucent and without color. " 'Tis why I must do all I can for your father. What he did for my mother—why, she was so good and kind, and very beautiful before she grew ill. I was her only child, and she loved me."

Jonah recalled a young girl, not quite a woman, always taking in laundry to earn enough money whilst other girls attended husking bees and socials and teas, did charity work, or were being courted by young men. He knew now her harshness was meant to drive away those who teased her for being so distant, although he could see now it was her circumstances that kept her from what others her age had enjoyed.

"I remember your mother."

"You do?" How she lit up, like sunlight peering through trees, like hope coming to dark places.

"Aye. My best recollection is when I was ten and Thomas and I were put in the stocks for mischief and she was in the crowd with you."

"You were put there for throwing rocks at a cow. I remember. You were a horrible little boy. If only you had been punished for pulling my braids in dame school, you might not have turned to more serious crime."

"Aye, right you are. I wonder what the penalty would be now if I gave your hair a tug?"

"Tug on my braids and you will likely find yourself bottom first in that mud puddle up ahead."

"Some things never change. I recall landing in many a puddle or snow patch when I was young. And all because of you."

"Well, you deserved it."

They laughed together, and how good it felt. But then the curving road twisted around a final corner, and she saw grandfather's stout wooden house. All the brief gaiety faded. She did not want to go home. Gray smoke crept from the stone chimney in a lazy curl, and she wondered if the morning meal was waiting for her, or, if not, a messy kitchen.

No matter that Jonah could make her laugh or had proposed marriage to her in the frosty air, this was her life. She did not like it, but she could not change it. A wedding promise was binding by law.

Nay, it was best to put her feet back on the ground and keep them there where they belonged. She could not be pining after a man she could not have. How her family would laugh if they knew she harbored a secret want for the heroic major. "Thank you for the cloak. I know it was your mother's, and I will cherish it."

She stepped down and hurried around the horses, not daring to raise her eyes to see if he was sad or relieved.

The front door snapped open and Grandfather's short rotund figure filled the frame. "Horace stopped by to retrieve his ironing. I told him you would be here at suppertime to take care of it. Hurry up, work is waiting."

Tessa felt shame creep across her face, shame because she knew Jonah watched and listened. She could feel his gaze heavy on her back. She did not want to know what he thought, what opinion he formed.

If Jonah Hunter harbored tender feelings for her, as he claimed, they surely would be changed now that he saw her life, saw what she was to become: Horace Walling's wife.

Tears burned in her throat and she raced around the back of the house before anyone could see them fall.

He watched her avoid him that evening when she returned, after tending to her chores at home, to sit by Father's side. She kept to herself, her chin down, shielded by the fall of dark curls across her face. She kept him and Andy running after more wood and fresh water and clean towels until the moon slid behind dark clouds and there was nothing but darkness.

Aye, he'd made a mistake proposing to her. No doubt about it.

"Let me guess, all did not go well with Mistress Tessa this afternoon." Thomas poured two cups of coffee at the hearth, a smirk shaping his usually serious mouth.

"Do not dare laugh at me. I have had a bad enough day as it is." Jonah snatched the sugar bowl from the shelf and set it on the table. There were so many cakes and baked goods it was hard to find room. "How many women visited today?"

"I would say nearly thirty. Some were already married and just being neighborly."

"Aye, but how many looking for a wedding ring?"

"Twenty, mayhap."

"And not one offered to look after Father."

"Ah, so now you see the flaw in your logic." Thomas shook his head as he carried the steaming cups from the hearth. "Tell me, Tessa Bradford didn't accept."

"Nay."

"She could not. Rumor has it she is to marry Horace Walling next Sunday."

"She is merely betrothed."

"Aye, but you have been gone from Baybrooke too long. You have forgotten how binding those agreements are. Which is why I'm extremely careful whom I propose to."

With a wry wink, Thomas set the cups on a free corner of the table and dropped into a chair. "What will you do about Father? He has not shown much improvement. The doctor came this afternoon whilst you were away. You know he holds little hope. It saddens me, but 'Tis only a matter of time until Father passes."

"And little time for me to keep my vows." He did not need reminding. Jonah shoveled a few heaping spoonfuls of sugar into his cup and stirred, considering.

"How will you choose another woman?"

"I don't want another. I have to figure out how to keep the one I have."

"What?" Thomas spilled coffee down the front of his shirt. "Damn. I can't believe you had all evening to reconsider and you still want her."

"Then tell me what I should do?"

"Marry a more agreeable woman. Tessa does not know her place, as a proper woman should. She's been a spinster too long. I fear you've made a mistake, brother."

"A mistake? Why, you wagered Andy five pounds over my mistake."

Thomas groaned. "Do not remind me, brother. I'm not proud of myself. I only meant to jest. Why, Tessa is an honest enough woman, but there isn't one man in all of Connecticut Colony who wouldn't blame you for choosing another."

Troubled, Jonah faced the window, studying the night-black windowpanes and his own reflection within.

"Besides, she is too much like our stepmother, sharp-tongued and harsh. Can't you at least remember how our stepmother nearly destroyed our father? With one sharp-tongued demand after another. And her suffocating selfishness."

"Tessa is not selfish." Jonah spun from the window. "She is always compassionate and tender with Father. She would never harm another."

" 'Tis you that I'm worried about." Trouble darkened Thomas' brow. "How will you handle such a woman? She is not sweet and biddable."

"Nay, but she's the only woman I can see myself in bed with." Amazed at his frankness, Jonah paused.

Thomas stared open-mouthed. "So, I see. Been sampling the goods?"

Not as much as he would like to. Jonah felt heat creep across his face and desire pulse through his blood. Tessa's kisses had tasted as seductive as the night. He wanted her. All of her. Every night in his bed. She would give him the son he needed.

"She is an upstanding woman," Thomas agreed. "Above reproach morally. Why, there's no doubt she's an untried virgin. Between her mother's long illness and then serving in Ely Bradford's home, she has had no spare time for dalliances of any kind."

"Trust me, Tessa is no untried virgin." Not a woman who kissed as she did.

"It cannot be so! Why, I know of no man who would—"

"Some man has. And I'm determined to be the next one to lift her skirts."

He watched his brother's face slacken and the regret creep into the creases at his eyes. The very air seemed to change. Thomas cleared his throat. "Good evening, Mistress Tessa."

She saw how Jonah turned around in his chair, dread clear on his face. He looked guilty and apologetic, but his words still rang in her ears. She had been wrong to let him kiss her, to let her own desire for such a man overshadow her better judgment "I have your father settled for the night. I'll be back to check on him after midnight. I have some business to attend to."

"Would you like a ride home?" Jonah stood abruptly, and his chair scraped against the wood floor. " 'Tis cold outside tonight."

"As it has been all winter. I will be fine. Stay with your father, who needs you." She grabbed her old cloak from the peg by the back door, the bloodstain prominent and the patches new. "Excuse me."

The cold wind felt good on her face. She hadn't wanted to come here this night. For once she wanted to stay and work in her grandfather's home because she wanted to avoid seeing Jonah. She never wanted to lay eyes on him again. No matter how hot his kisses or how he made her dream.

She broke into a run when she reached the road and kept on going.

"I think she overheard." Thomas set aside his cup.

"I know she did. She would have to be deaf not to hear." He rubbed his hands across his face. Lord, what had he done? How much had she heard?

"We can hire a couple of nurses." Thomas turned his attention to a plate of cornbread. "Father will have care, you can pick a better woman, and you will be free of this harebrained idea of yours. No one will offer to help with Father, Jonah."

"Tessa did."

"You said yourself she has a lover. And you plan to be next. That doesn't have to change."

"That's not what I meant." Jonah snatched his cup and carried it to the board counter and stacked it beside the other dirty dishes. "I have decided on Tessa. Accept my decision, Thomas."

" 'Tis your choice. You will have to live with her a long while. Just consider that."

"I have." He had done nothing but think of it all day. He'd watched her move around the house, slim and graceful and as proper as could be, but he knew different. He'd caught a glimpse of her passionate nature, had tasted her seasoned kisses, and knew the rest of her would be as sweet.

He pulled back the curtain to watch Tessa, but she was nowhere in sight. If she had been heading home, she would have cut across their backyard, taking the way through the woods. He headed toward the parlor, where only a single bayberry candle tossed a weak light across polished floors and furniture.

He tugged back the draperies and gazed out into the darkness. Fog misted the ground and obscured much of the road. Damn, where did she go? Then he saw a faint movement, nothing more than a shadow.

Wherever she was headed, it wasn't toward home. Jonah remembered how he'd come across her his first night in town, alone in the woods. No decent woman crept around in the dark like that. And never alone.

He grabbed his coat and headed out into the night. Cold crept through his clothes, but he kept walking. She moved quickly, and once again he lost sight of her. Soon, his eyes adjusted to the thick bleak darkness and he caught sight of her again, nearly running full out down the rutted lane.

The fool woman was going to twist an ankle in one of those ruts or slide on the ice. And worse, who was her lover that she ran so fast for the comfort of his arms? Jonah had no doubt the day had been difficult for her. She still believed she was bound by law and ethics to wed Horace Walling.

Jonah wasn't big on ethics and he didn't give a damn for the law. Whatever it cost him, that drunken wife-beater would not walk down the same road as Tessa Bradford, let alone call her wife. He had seen how she was treated at home by a grandfather more moved by greed than family bonds. This woman, who cared for Father with such tenderness and honor-bound devotion.

Only one question remained in his mind, and it had been troubling him since the morning. Who was her lover?

He followed her to a grove of maples where a path cut off the road. Her shoes left clear tracks in the snow. He kept back, so she would not know he followed her. She glanced over her shoulder several times but hadn't seen him. He made sure of it.

She stopped at the edge of the pond, frozen and dark. 'Twas as if she expected to meet someone. She dropped to her knees at the water's edge, now nothing but a dark sheen of thick ice, and put her face to her hands. The faintest sound of tears, of racking heart-deep sobs carried on the wind.

His heart cracked in two. Lord, she was crying. Hard and unrestrained, thinking she was alone. He could guess what troubled her. She'd barely spoken to him today, and then she would not meet his gaze.

She thought he cared for her, and she'd said it herself. She wanted to marry him. But she was already bound by oath and a paid dowry to another man. He hadn't considered how his proposal might hurt her feelings. Surely she could see the solution as easily as he did.

Her tears did not cease, her sobs did not fade. Every bit of his soul wanted to step out into the clearing and go to her. He wanted to hold her tight against his chest until her crying stopped. He wanted to tell her he would pay Horace Walling whatever he wanted, but the agreement between him and her grandfather would be broken.

Father had little time and besides, Jonah wanted no other. Tessa was the right choice. She would not make his life hell, not as their stepmother had done. He knew in his heart that Thomas was wrong. The notorious spinster of Baybrooke was little more than a tender mouse inside, and a woman capable of great passion.

Time passed, and he stood shivering, waiting. Finally her tears stopped. The moon peered out from between thick clouds to glow on the shadowed snow. She wiped her face and stood, then stepped out on the ice. She ran and slid and twirled with her hands out, gaining speed and momentum.

Jonah stepped out of the shelter of the grove, amazed at the sight. Her hair had come down and trailed behind her, sailing and shimmering as dark as the night, and she looked so free, so different from the dutiful woman who had hurried to her grandfather's stables or the angel of mercy who cared all night for his father.

She had been playing on the ice that night he'd come across her. Not meeting a lover. There was no sign of anyone in these peaceful woods, solemn and silent except for Tessa's joy as she slid and frolicked.

His heart cracked, and he hated interrupting her. He suspected her life was severe and held no joy, except for this one freedom, this way she sailed across the frozen pond.

"Tessa."

"*Jonah.*" She lost her balance and hit the ice hard. She spun to a stop on her rump. "What are you doing here?"

"I followed you."

"Why? Oh, I know. You thought I might let you lift my skirts next after I entertained my first lover?" The words tasted so bitter.

"Nay." How sad he sounded. "I only wanted to see who you met with."

"Why, so you can ruin my life further?" She climbed up off the ice. "I heard what you said to your brother."

"Go ahead and get angry at me. Then give me a chance to apologize."

He actually looked contrite. Tessa would have laughed if it didn't hurt so much. She fisted her hands and sorely wished she believed in violence. She would give that man a good smack to the head for what he'd put her through today. Proposing to her! And now this. He almost had her believing—

"You're crying again." He sounded surprised.

"What do you think I would do, enjoy being made sport of? Just like in school when you teased me and pulled on my braids?"

"I did it because I thought you were pretty."

"Except, I'm not pretty. Don't start with the lies. I can take anything tonight but more lies." She stalked off the ice, skirting him intentionally. She didn't trust her self-control right now. Her fist might somehow accidentally connect with his jaw.

"You are bad tempered, but pretty. I have always thought so."

How sincere he sounded. "What do you think? That you can sweet talk me into pulling up my skirts for you? Is that why you're here? Is that why you proposed to me?"

"Tessa, you seem overset. Why don't you calm down—"

Overset! Before she could stop her hand, it was scooping up a fistful of snow. Anger blasted red before her eyes and she aimed and threw. "If you think I'm overset, you just wait."

He sidestepped, but the snowball hit him square in the forehead. "Damn it, why in blazes did you hit me?"

"Why? You have to ask why?" She sent another snowball sailing at his head. He managed to dodge this one, but her anger flared higher, hotter. "Maybe you don't understand, because a big brute of a man like you, who has everybody worshipping every step you take, probably doesn't have a single feeling in that big old swelled head of yours. But when something hurts me, I feel it."

"You're right." He held out his hand. "Please, no more snowballs."

"Maybe I should try using a stick on that head of yours."

He laughed, a deep gravelly sound. "Fine. I'm big and stupid. End of argument."

"Well, I'm far from done. The only reason I even stepped foot inside your house tonight is because of your father. He's a nice man, unlike his ungrateful son.

"True." He stalked after her, swift and as cunning as a wolf. He seemed more shadow than substance. "I am not arguing. You're right and I'm wrong."

"What's this? The great Jonah Hunter is being agreeable? I can't imagine why. Wait, I think I know. And let me tell you right now that I'm not going to let you lift my skirts—"

"If you are my wife, you will." A smile flirted along his mouth. "I made an offer to you today, and as far as I'm concerned it still stands."

Tightness filled her chest. "You offered to marry me. But you know full well why I can't."

"Why not? You said you wanted me."

Panic tore through her chest. "I said no such thing. I would never want a man like you."

"A man like me. You say that often." Something snapped in his eyes, intriguing and spellbinding enough to steal her breath away. "You seem to know much about men like me."

"Not as much as you think."

"Maybe you aren't as innocent as you seem." He halted before her, so big he was all she could see. "Mayhap I should find out for certain."

Tessa caught her breath as he laid a hand against her jaw. Heat pulsed across her skin and beat through her blood. This man wanted her? Loved her? She could not see it in his eyes, but it was there in his touch. So hot and possessive and tender all at once, it had to be love.

"Aw, Tessa." Desire for her flickered in his eyes. "You are a dangerous woman."

"Mayhap that is why all the bachelors in the village avoid me."

Laughter flirted along his mouth. "I will have to be very careful around you."

"Because I'm so dangerous?"

He puzzled her, filled her up, and left her dizzy. How could a man do that, affect her in such a way? Her entire body felt alive as it pulsed and tingled, and all for him. She didn't think she loved him, but she did want him, did feel something for him. And it tingled in her blood and buzzed on her lips.

"You're dangerous because you make me forget to think." His mouth captured hers.

The chunk of snow she still held slipped from her hand and clattered to the icy ground. The night seemed to silence as his kiss deepened and his hold on her tightened. He tasted like a cold winter night and something deeper, hotter, more thrilling. His tongue traced the seam of her lips, his hands cradled her neck. She tipped her head back, opening her mouth, accepting the intimate caress of his tongue.

How strangely wondrous. He was all velvet heat, warm and heady, and she surrendered to him completely. His hands smoothed down her back, sending tingling waves of pleasure through her spine. Then up the side of her ribs, dangerously close to her breasts.

Jonah backed her against a tree trunk and trapped her there with the breadth of his magnificent chest and the strength in his body. She didn't mind at all, not when he could make her feel like this. She feathered her fingers across the span of his shoulders. How could a man feel like heaven? He was hard muscle and strength and her fingers ached to touch more.

On a moan, Jonah wrapped his arms around her and hauled her hard against him. She felt every plane of him, every hardness. Her blood pulsed down low in her stomach, and lower still.

He tore away from the kiss, his breathing ragged. Want glazed his eyes, and even in the thick darkness broken only by a dusting of moonlight, she could see how he wanted her, how he desired only her.

She leaned back against the knobby tree trunk, struggling to catch her breath. It was impossible. Jonah just kept gazing down at her, then he reached out and his fingers caught the collar of her cloak. He tugged and buttons came free.

Before she could think to stop him, he smoothly loosened the wooden buttons on the front of her dress. Just four, and he slid his hand beneath the placket. The heat from his fingers seared through her wool underwear. He plundered those buttons too, never lifting his gaze from hers.

"Jonah, you mustn't do this." She breathed the words.

"I already am." His fingers brushed the soft inside curve of her left breast.

A sharp gasp drew her up. "But what about my betrothal?"

"By this time tomorrow, it will no longer exist. Trust me." His clever fingers molded the curve of her breast and began kneading.

On a sigh, she tipped back her head, exposing the long elegant column of her throat Cascades of black curls shimmered with Stardust, and he'd never seen anything so beautiful. She tossed her head to one side and then the other. With a moan, she arched her back and pressed the soft heat of her breasts into the palms of his hands. Soft light brushed her face, accenting the bow of her mouth, so relaxed with pleasure. He'd never seen such an enchantress.

She was a danger, this one. She could reach right in and grab hold of his heart. Blood liquefied in his veins, so hot and molten it thrummed in his groin, and his shaft pulsed hard and taut.

He tugged at more buttons, revealing her perfect flesh to the silvered moonlight. Sweet heaven, but she was a sight. Creamy white, her breasts, softly rounded, and pink tipped. She fit perfectly into his hands.

"Oh, Jonah," she breathed, her fingers curling around his upper arms, digging into his muscles.

Need punched through his body. His groin felt heavy and aching. She looked so ready, with her head tipped back and her eyes closed, making tiny moans as he slipped one hand down her abdomen to inch up her skirts.

Forgotten were the reasons he'd come. He adored the firmness of her breasts, so ripe he wanted to taste them. He bent down, intending to draw one generous nipple into his mouth.

But her hands caught his wrists, stopping him. "I hear something."

The words were whispers, spoken so raggedly he could hardly understand her. "Probably just my heart."

It was pounding like a war drum. All he could think of was finding his way beneath her skirts and burying his aching shaft deep within her willing body.

"Jonah—" The warning sharpened. She clutched her dress over her breasts, covering them.

Ely Bradford stood in the clearing, his gun in one hand. "I ought to shoot you where you stand, Hunter. My granddaughter has an agreement with my neighbor and good friend. She is not your property."

"Not yet." Jonah stood in front of Tessa while she fumbled with the buttons. Something wet struck his hand.

Her tears. With chin down, he couldn't read her face, but a warning went off in his head. Tessa Bradford was as tough as stone and twice as cold, or so many people said.

"You and I have much to discuss, Ely." Jonah turned his back on the man. He stared at Tessa's tears.

Her clothes straight, she lifted her chin. Heat stained her face. Shadows made her eyes black.

She was embarrassed. No, ashamed. Maybe Tessa wasn't as experienced as he thought.

CHAPTER NINE

Rain dripped from the eaves and beat at the outside walls of the attic, but Tessa refused to let the dreary weather dim her spirits. It was her wedding day.

"He sent his brother to come get your things," Violet huffed as she stormed into the tiny bedchamber. "Notice that he must not have wanted to come himself."

Tessa took one look at the triumphant malice on the girl's face. It had been no secret that everyone in the household had thought Violet held a good chance of being the major's choice for a bride. She kept her voice low. "His father is gravely ill. Jonah rarely leaves his side."

"He did to be alone with you in the woods." Violet's lip curled. "To compromise you. Everyone is talking about it. And wondering how many men there have been over the years."

Tessa clamped her jaw shut and tamped down her anger. She would not let the vicious girl rile her on this special day. She was getting married, something she had wished for on endless first stars of the night

And to a man who would not be abusive or cruel, to one who made her blood heat and her heart pitter-patter. *She* was marrying the most eligible bachelor in the whole of Baybrooke village. She, Tessa Bradford.

"Tell Thomas I'll be right down." Tessa turned her back and

knelt to secure the old trunk's clasp.

"I'm hardly your servant." Violet's words came sharp, dripping with unveiled hatred. "There is only one reason why Major Hunter has agreed to marry you, and everyone knows it. And it isn't because you were caught with your bodice down. 'Tis because he wants you to take care of his father."

"He could hire ten women far more skilled than I am to tend his father. Everyone knows that, too." She held her chin firm and refused to let Violet's mean words bother her, even if the same thought had occurred to her last night when sleep would not come and she was remembering Jonah's touch, Jonah's passion.

"But some services he cannot hire here in the good township of Baybrooke, as last night proved. Why else would he risk getting caught trying to rut with you? Why else would he want an ugly, sharp-faced old hen when he could have—"

Heavy footsteps knelled in the tiny landing outside the attic room. A man cleared his voice.

Tessa stood to face Thomas Hunter, who was too tall to straighten to his full height outside her tiny bedchamber. "Thomas, I thought to bring the trunk down myself. The ladder is hard to manage."

"I've climbed ladders before carrying heavier items than your small trunk." He looked uncomfortable and his mouth crooked down in the corners. "Are you ready?"

"Aye. I just need to grab my cloak downstairs."

"Then go on down. I will follow with the trunk." He somehow molded his big body against the wall so she could pass.

"You did not need to come. I could have managed—"

"You are family now. The Hunters help their own." His words were cold, but his dark gaze was kind when he looked at her. Then he flicked his head upward to stare harshly at Violet.

"Mr. Hunter." Violet primped her lustrous curls with one soft hand. "How magnificent to have such an esteemed member of the community in our very own house."

" 'Tis a dubious honor at best."

Violet's flirting sagged, and she blinked several times, her jaw slackening.

Turning to climb down the rickety ladder, Tessa tried to hide her smile. She hurried out of Violet's way, who was barreling down after her, her anger at Thomas' insult barely disguised.

"Tessa." A deep bass welcomed from the parlor, proving Violet wrong.

"Jonah." He'd come. Every muscle in her body tensed. The air caught sideways in her throat.

He stood smack in the middle of the room, broad shoulders set, booted feet braced apart. Untamed black hair, windblown and lashed by the rain, framed his strong cut face. A black waistcoat draped his solidly planed chest, and dark breeches hugged his well-muscled thighs.

Fire licked to life inside Tessa's chest. Why was it this man who sent shivers down her spine and heat through her veins? "I did not think to see you before the ceremony."

"Surprise." His gaze raked hers boldly and a brazen grin stretched his mouth, not full-fledged, but just a hint of one, and she had no doubt he was remembering how he'd kissed her and caressed her breasts in the faint light of the moon.

She tingled deep inside at the memory, at the knowledge that he was thinking of it too. And grinning.

"Your grandfather and I have come to an agreement concerning your dowry."

"I didn't know you were expecting one." She flashed her gaze to Grandfather, who stood grave and dour-faced near the parlor's crackling hearth. "Surely there is not much to offer ..."

Charity made a gasping sound in the corner, where Violet now huddled beside her. "A much-used bride is worth naught, I can tell you."

A much-used bride. Tessa closed her eyes, willing down the anger before it erupted. Let them think what they wanted. She knew the truth. And so did Jonah. She was a virgin still, yet her stepgrandmother's words did pierce like a well-sharpened edge of a blade.

"I am well enough satisfied," Grandfather grunted, arms crossed over his chest. Despite his unhappy expression, she saw the glint of greed in his eyes, a mostly veiled look of contentment. "All I want is for you to get out of my house before your reckless ways and evil tongue tarnish our good family's name for eternity."

"Amen to that." Charity's shrill voice rang with contempt. "We have Violet's reputation to think of. How many eligible bachelors have refused even to consider her because she is related to you?"

Tessa's stomach roiled at Charity and Violet's accusing gazes.

Did they blame her because Jonah did not propose to Violet? She suspected they did.

"Now, Mistress Bradford, a gentle tongue is more becoming than a forked one." Jonah purred the insult so that it sounded less offensive, but all the more effective.

Charity's mouth snapped shut with a click of teeth.

Tessa's chest filled as he extended his hand to her, palm up, powerful and yet infinitely tender. His big fingers curled around hers and gently guided her close to him, not touching, but close enough so that she could smell the wondrous woodland scent of him and see the dark flecks of black in his spellbinding eyes. Anger sizzled there, controlled but definite.

"Come, the good reverend will be at our house in one hour."

"What? You're not marrying in the meetinghouse?" Charity sounded appalled.

"Nay, my father is too ill to leave his bed, and he wishes to see the ceremony." With a half-grin, half-frown shaping his face, he stalked to the front door.

Thomas clomped down the narrow staircase from the second story, after apparently successfully negotiating the attic ladder, her small trunk balanced easily on one capable shoulder.

Jonah jerked open the door and held it for her. She snatched her cloak from the peg, and her heart soared at the tug of his hands on the garment, helping her into it. The way he treated her in front of her family made her want to run out into the yard and shriek for joy.

She was finally rid of those people who had caused her an unrelenting unhappiness, who had been so cruel to her mother.

And yet, as Jonah followed her out into the cold rain and the mess of mud and melting snow, she had to wonder. Was she trading one kind of unhappiness for another?

She'd vowed long ago only to marry for love, and even then always to keep her independence, for she would never forget her mother's unhappiness or the lessons of her death.

As Jonah placed both big hands at her waist to boost her up into his wagon, she could not meet his gaze, could not bear to look at his handsome face. Her body reacted to his touch, swift and hard, and heat spilled into her veins and spread through her abdomen.

She was making a grave mistake. She knew it with an unerring certainty as she settled her skirts on the seat. And yet there was no mistaking how Jonah cared for her.

Love you, he'd said, low and barely audible, and his remembered words melted her heart.

Panic mounted with each step of the horse. When he arrived home, they would marry, he and Tessa. Marry. Damn, how that set his heart a-beating. He fought the urge to toss down the reins and run.

Be reasonable, he told himself. Surely this is a logical reaction to impending matrimony. All men must feel the same way, like a coward, wanting to flee after realizing the permanency of such an act.

Tessa sat beside him, her face bowed against the rain. He could see little of it for the brim of her old hat, but the tight curve of her clenched jaw told him she was having fears too.

He didn't fool himself. He'd feel this way about marrying any female. Love was a ridiculous emotion, one that could not exist in a heart lost long ago on a bloody battlefield. He had seen the true nature of life, of death and brutality, and he ought to take comfort that his bride was no green girl, head full of silly and romantic notions. Tessa was a woman of duty.

Aye, there was a small squeeze to his heart when he looked at her. Thomas had told him of the small chamber she lived in, tucked beneath the roof, as cold and damp as a chicken hut, barely large enough to hold a small pallet and her old trunk. The poor woman had no real bed.

The burning anger in his chest flickered to life again. Ely was a squinty-eyed weasel. And the money Jonah had handed over to appease both him and Horace Walling made him sick inside. Not at the loss of such a substantial chunk of coin, but because the old man had acted as if Tessa was a cow to be sold.

The house loomed up ahead, a gray shape in the gloom of the unrelenting rain. "Are you thinking of running off the minute I stop this wagon?"

She nodded, turning just enough toward him so that he could see the luminous depth of her eyes, filled with worry, pinched with fear. "Aye. It did cross my mind."

"Mine, too." It comforted him that she was as uncertain as he. That showed she had sense, that he had not judged wrongly. She knew marriage was duty, not romance for starry-eyed lovers. "I told Father the news this morning when he asked why you hadn't come to tend him."

"Jonah, I should have come."

" 'Twas best this way. I had time alone with him, as I've been wanting, and you needed to pack. You shall never return to that household again."

Something bright and wondrous gleamed in Tessa's eyes, so compelling he could not look away. "Thank you, Jonah. You don't know what that means to me."

Complaints and heartache, even anger, went unspoken. Rain tapped steadily between them, the sound multiplied a thousand times across the yard as Jonah halted the wagon. One of the horses exhaled loudly, mayhap protesting the weather.

"Here we are." Jonah handed the reins to his brother, who had already agreed to tend to the horses so that he might be able to take care of his bride. "I'll take your trunk up to my chamber."

"Oh." Her eyes widened. She paled suddenly, as if struck ill. Or realizing that tonight they would share a bed.

Heat thrummed in his groin. The thought of her naked beneath him, her head thrown back in passion made his pulse jump, made him want, just want. He would never forget the heady taste of her passion-laced kiss or the little catch in her breath when he'd first touched her breasts. He wanted to hear that sound again, right now. He wanted to see her with candlelight brushing her full breasts. He wanted her naked and out of control and all his.

Somehow, he managed to help her down from the wagon and shouldered her trunk from the back of the wagon bed. He followed her through the parlor and up the stairs to his chamber down the hall. She didn't meet his gaze as she stood before the window, the gray light limning her lean woman's curves and the sensual luxury of her dark hair.

His groin thrummed, and his breeches felt unusually tight. Aye, he wanted her. Tonight she would be his. "The reverend should be here within the next half hour."

She looked at him with eyes wide with apprehension. "I need to change into my dress."

He set the trunk along the wall by the door and tried not to imagine how she would peel off that dark sensible dress and reveal the soft firm breasts beneath.

"I'll leave you alone, then." He turned before he imagined undressing her further. "I need to check on Father."

She merely nodded, her arms wrapped tight around her middle. He left her then, his shaft bent double in his breeches, hard and pulsing, and closed the door.

Tonight would not be soon enough to make her his.

"Jonah," Father called, weak and thin sounding.

"I'm here." Taking a breath, he tried to will away the very pulse of his blood, then crossed the hall. The chamber still smelled of sickness—a weak, low scent that reminded him of midnight.

Father struggled to turn his head on the pillows. "You caught me reading. The good news of your wedding has helped me improve. I believe I can almost sit up."

"Mayhap I can read to you, as long as you stay lying down." Jonah pulled the wooden chair close to the bed, concern and tenderness for this man warm in his chest.

" 'Twould be a great comfort. 'Tis a new volume of poetry by John Donne."

"Hand me the book. Where is Andy? I thought he would have offered to read to you."

Father's hands trembled with terrible weakness as he handed over the slim, leather-bound book. "Seeing to hiring a few village women for a celebration dinner. Since we lost Sarah when her term was done, we are in sore need of help. We can't expect Tessa to wait upon all four of us men. Not if you get her with child soon."

"Aye, the son you expect of me." Jonah cracked open the book with practiced care.

Dark eyes glimmered. "Have you bedded her yet, boy?"

"*What?*"

Father's laughter, punctuated by a cough or two, filled the room with his happiness. "I may be a sick old man staring death straight in the face, but I'm sharp enough yet to recognize certain things. I remember what lust looks like. And feels like, too."

"You heard how Ely came upon us last night."

"Aye, no doubt the entire village knows. Tessa is a wise choice in a wife, good and kind. And if you cannot keep your hands off her, 'Tis even better. A warm wife in bed makes for a contented husband."

"More of your wisdom, eh?" Jonah leafed past the title page of the volume.

"You chose well." Father closed his eyes. "Read to me, son."

Jonah began reading aloud, hearing the tightness in his own voice. And as the clock ticked patiently on the mantle above the fire, he felt his bachelorhood slip away. It was much to surrender, but his father had asked this of him. So he would marry Tessa and hope for the best

"Tessa, Reverend Brown is here." A knock rattled the closed door.

"I'll be right out." She gave her hair one more brush stroke. Her worries had turned into a full-fledged panic. Only the thought of returning to Grandfather's home kept her steady enough to open the door.

Jonah held out his hand. "Come. Father is waiting."

He was a man used to issuing orders and having them followed, a war hero, a leader of men. Her heart stammered at the sight of him.

"I suppose no one in my family has arrived." She laid her fingers against his palm, rough and callused but solid and comforting and oh, so hot.

"Nay. Ely proclaimed he did not approve of the union, especially since he discovered me with my hands down your bodice." A wry grin twisted his mouth, and pleasure snapped in his eyes.

Oh, he looked proud of himself for that. "I never should have allowed you such liberties. Else you could be marrying a more suitable bride."

He halted at the head of the stairs. One dark brow quirked. "Is that what you think? That I'm forced to take you as my wife?"

She swallowed and nodded.

"Tessa." His voice melted, like butter before heat, supple and warm. "I can think of no other I could stomach as well as you for my wife."

"Aye, so now you make jokes."

"Well, we need a jest to relieve this tension. Besides, I don't want a silly child for a wife. We went to school together, and I survived your sharp tongue."

"As I survived your braid pulling."

"I say we shall do fine enough in a marriage." His dark eyes sizzled, stroking across her breasts with a glittering look of anticipation. "I have sampled enough to expect good things to come."

"Aye, you *are* a devil's spawn." She blushed, her stomach tumbling to her knees. This man was trouble, pure and simple. And yet he was her best chance for a real future, for marriage and happiness and children.

He cared for her enough to pay Grandfather and Horace Walling, enough to marry her. Not every man who ruined a woman's reputation offered her his last name. Jonah cared for her, and that thought fortified her. Made it easier to flash him a smile as they descended into the parlor where the minister waited.

"Let us start this ceremony before both of us drop dead from the anxiety."

"Brace yourself, Mistress Tessa." Thomas caught her hand to wish her luck. "You're marrying a rogue no other woman would have."

She laughed, for his eyes teased. "Aye, I know. 'Tis a foolhardy thing I do, but mayhap it will earn me a spot in heaven for marrying such a toad."

"An ugly toad, no less," Andy piped up.

"Enough." Jonah boomed, holding up one hand. "Stay the insults. Make fun all you want after the ceremony. I have a great need to make this woman my wife."

His arm slipped around her waist, and they faced the minister together. Laughter filled the elegant parlor, despite the gray weather outside, despite the solemn occasion.

"Dearly beloved," the reverend began and the room quieted so that the tick of the clock sounded loud, louder than the rain tapping at the diamond paned windows, even louder than the erratic beat of her heart.

With the simple words of "I do," and a kiss so hot her toes felt afire, she became Mrs. Jonah Hunter.

"He's asleep." Jonah knelt at the old man's bedside, next to his quiet wife, merely a shadow sitting out of reach of the single taper's light. "Andy will stay with him the rest of the night."

Her eyes widened, and she knew what he was thinking. What had to come next? He had bided his time all afternoon and evening, blood zinging through his veins, knowing she was to be his. He could not explain this physical desire for her, but it grew in intensity with every breath he took.

The knowledge of what was to come shadowed her face. So dark they were, lustrous and inviting. So dark the pupils in her eyes. Luminous with desire. "The colonel is exhausted from today's excitement. I don't want to take my eyes off him."

"Andy will fetch us if there's any sign of trouble."

A rustle sounded from the chair by the fireplace. "Aye, I will. Jonah has already spoken to me."

He shot a warning look at his younger brother, who was still half horrified in his choice of wife. Jonah had made it clear to both brothers he and Tessa were to have their privacy tonight.

With the way the urgency beat in his blood, he was already hard with wanting her. So much want. So very hard. And all she did was look at him.

Aye, Father was right. He would not mind the binds of marriage overmuch with Tessa to satisfy him. She smiled faintly, her chin wobbling. Aye, she must be feeling this need too. He remembered how she had tossed her head when he'd stroked the peaks of her breasts, and how she arched her back, readily offering up those sweet dusky nipples.

Fie on Ely for interrupting him. But that would not happen tonight. Need wrapped around his lower spine, swift and keen. He took Tessa's hand in his and stood.

She did as well. She had changed out of the soft beige gown of her mother's and now wore a somber homespun dress. The dark fabric shivered around her hips and thighs when she stood. Such a sensuous movement, supple and light. He had no doubt that was the way Tessa would behave in his bed, head thrown back, arching up to meet him.

"Come." He cleared his throat, but his voice sounded husky to his own ears. " 'Tis time to retire for the night."

In the corner, Andy blushed and turned to face the fire. Mayhap he did not see the true nature of Tessa Bradford the way Jonah did.

"Andy, make certain to steep the tea at midnight and again at three in the morning. 'Tis a medicine that will aid his recovery." She brushed at her skirts, a nervous gesture.

Andy made some grunt of agreement, still red-faced. Jonah held back his chuckle at the young man who was more sheltered than the rest of the Hunter brothers.

He held open the door for Tessa, then followed her out into the hall. The shadows and darkness swallowed her, but her hand was warm within his. "I have been thinking of this all day."

"So have I." She sounded shy, and he liked that.

"I have not forgotten our night together in the forest." He led her to his chamber—theirs, now— and released her hand so he could light a taper. Just one, 'twould be enough to see her by.

"Do you regret it?" A weak flame flickered to life, revealing the wide depth of her eyes.

"Only that we could not finish what we started." He still remembered how free she was, this woman renowned for her sharp tongue and no-nonsense attitude. How well she had hidden her true nature all these years, passion smoldering beneath dark homespun.

A spark of want blazed to life in his chest, brazen and possessive, building with each beat of his heart. That passion would be his, as she was his, now and forever.

She had retreated to the corner of the room, cloaked in shadows near the window where a constant rain tapped at the glass. So, she was shy, preferring darkness to the light. Well, he would soon fix that.

"Come, show me your wanton nature." He curled one hand around her nape, the silken luxury of her curls teasing his knuckles, and the heat of her skin scorched his palm. " 'Tis what I crave."

"Jonah," she breathed, as his mouth descended on hers.

He tasted the sweetness of his name on her lips. She was heated satin, and he was spellbound. He flicked his tongue across the seam of her mouth and she opened up to him with a tentative brush of her tongue to his.

Fire streaked through his chest, burning hotter, brighter. Aye, she responded to him, molding her lips to his, licking and sucking. She was but a temptress. The flames in his chest built until every part of him felt on fire, until he laid his hands on her breasts, despite the barrier of cotton, and kneaded and rubbed.

On a moan, she arched into his touch, head falling back. Hell, but she was going to destroy him. Already his hands shook with want, his body trembled with every pulse of his beating heart, and his shaft stretched his breeches to the limit.

He tugged hard at her collar and the wooden buttons at her nape gave in one swift ripple, leaving the fabric loose around her shoulders. He licked his way down her neck, feasting on the salty sweetness of her skin and her throaty moans, dragging the fabric down with him. The straps of her chemise slipped easily down her creamy shoulders to reveal breasts shadowed and untouched by light. But not by him.

He dragged one pebbled nipple into his mouth, and she groaned low, breathing his name.

"Oh, Jonah. Yes." Her hair cascaded over her shoulders to brush at his cheek. She arched hard into him and her fingers wrapped around his neck to hold him there.

Pulse thundering in his ears, Jonah ran his tongue around the silken nub, taut and supple, and then suckled hard enough to made her gasp, to make her body tremble with hard coursing pleasure. Aye, he knew how it felt, to want, to ache. It was in her glazed eyes, dark and pooled with emotion. The same need beat within his veins and sparked the air between them.

Aye, he could wait no more. He gave her dress a mighty pull. One button popped and hit the wooden floor, rolling to a stop, and her garments slid down her hips to pool in a dark puddle at her ankles.

"Jonah, I don't think—"

"Don't think," he advised, as he scooped her up and laid her back on the bed. How bewitching she looked wearing only a set of drawers and her shoes. He knelt to take them off, and her stockings, too. "You know what I want. And thought has no place in what we're about to do."

He straddled over her, his knees on either side of her thighs, and tugged off his shirt. Aye, she was a beauty, lying within the brush of candlelight, her skin gleaming gold and her breasts firm and inviting. Her eyes darkened as she studied the breadth of his bare chest. So, she liked what she saw. He loosened his breeches, determined to show her more.

Hard as steel, his shaft sprang out How her gaze clamped onto that sight, her mouth opening slightly. Her intake of breath confirmed she had not been expecting so much of him.

"Is this what you have been thinking of too, seeing me like this?" He untied the bow at her waist and her drawers loosened. "For 'Tis all I have been wanting since we last met"

"Jonah?"

"What is it, sweet?" And how sweet she was. He parted fabric and discovered a softly curving belly, and below a thatch of dark hair.

"I know what happens, but—"

"But what?" Her thighs opened and his fingers parted delicate folds to discover dampness and heat.

"You're so very big." Her breath came swift and broken.

"Aye, and you'll like it, I promise." How wondrous she felt here, heat and satin, and his fingers explored the texture of her there, where the candlelight did not reach.

"Truly? I'm told there is much pain the first time."

His fingers continued to stroke and explore. She lay before him, thighs apart, naked and aroused and ready, so ready. "I'll be gentle. Do you like this?"

"Aye, your touches are good. So very good." A small grain of fear lived in her voice. But even more desire.

"Aye, 'Tis good." She looked so wanton, 'twas all he could do to keep himself from taking her now. " 'Twill feel even better, I promise."

"How could it possibly be better?" Pleasure glazed her eyes, and she felt liquid at his persistent caresses. "How long I have wanted you, just like this, and now you are ready." He stretched out over her, and he felt her sink more deeply into the mattress. "Show me how passionate you can be. I want to know that part of you."

"But I—"

He silenced her with a kiss, a fiery kiss that involved lips and teeth and tongue. He felt her body's reaction, for it was stretched full out beneath him. She strained up to take more of his kiss and her breasts pillowed his chest, her nipples scraping his chest hair. Her thighs parted just a bit, and he took advantage, pressing with the inside of his knees so she opened just for him.

"You like the feel of me, don't you?" The swollen head of his shaft thrummed against her dampness and heat.

"Jonah, 'Tis not what I expected." She gasped, fighting for breath and for control.

He could feel it too, how they were both on the edge. Blood thrummed through his veins, rich with want, pulsing with the strident need to bury every inch of his shaft inside her. Now. He could wait no longer. She was woman-hot and bewitching as he pressed into her, into the first welcome gloving of her body.

"Is this better than you expected?"

"Aye. How you're stretching me."

"And filling you up."

Slowly, now. He closed his eyes tight, determined to fight the thrumming pleasure daring him to plunge deeper, to take all he could from her. Aye, how he wanted to be sheathed completely in her silken heat. "I can feel how you like this."

" 'Tis so wondrous." Her words were broken, low and throaty. "Oh, Jonah."

Her head lolled back and he felt her body lift, her hips drive up to take more of him. Something gave and she gasped, and it was too late to take back control. He drove deep as she rose up to meet him. Sensation gripped the base of his spine and every inch she clenched within her. Pleasure that cut as sharp as a blade's edge made him call out, made him drive into her again and again.

She rose up to meet him with bold thrusts of her hips. Her hands snaked around his back to settle on his buttocks, clamping him to her as her ankles locked behind his hips. She moaned his name over and over again, and he could feel how close she was, the hard clamping of her muscles, the tremulous tension in her body. And then her release. Her head braced against his throat, her hips lifted, her body clenched in one wave after another.

He could not hold on. Tight punches of release struck low in his back and pulsed through his shaft, through every muscle and bone. He clenched his jaw, trying to keep in the cry of surrender, but he could not. His surrender, his possession of her was complete.

At the last pulse of his seed, he collapsed. All at once he was aware of her arms around his back, cradling him close, and her gentle kisses at his throat and chin.

"How you move me," he admitted, and then wished he could pull back the words.

Her smile became a kiss, and they started all over again.

CHAPTER TEN

Morning dawned with the weakest of light Tessa watched the darkness thin until a pale gray light played at the edges of the curtain. 'Twas so comfortable here in this big soft bed, and so warm with Jonah at her side.

Ah, to look at him took her breath away. He lay on his back, his long dark hair tumbled across the pristine pillowslips, his face relaxed in sleep, but the masculine intensity remained in the cut of his jaw and cheekbones. The covers puddled half way down his chest against bronzed skin faintly dusted with dark hair. How wide that chest was, and his shoulders too. One arm rested on his waist, the other somewhere beneath the blankets.

She lifted the covers carefully and then slid across the sheets quietly so as not to wake him. Sore muscles reminded her of last night's lovemaking. She blushed remembering how she'd responded to him, how thrilling it felt to be joined with him. How on earth did married people manage to look so dour faced and serious all the time? She felt like laughing out loud.

She changed into her favorite work dress, a light gray cotton she'd made herself. Tepid water that had once been warm sat in a pitcher on the corner commode. She washed her face, careful to keep the splashing to a minimum, but Jonah did not rouse. He lay still, his magnificent chest rising and falling with each breath.

She brushed out her hair quickly. She'd been a regular slug-a-bed this morning. Look, the sun was already rising. A rooster crowed somewhere, intent on announcing the arrival of the new day. Why, she had a house full of men to cook for. Between somber Thomas and terrified Andy, she wondered what they would think of her waltzing downstairs so late.

"Trying to escape me?" His voice came raw and husky from sleep. He smiled, low and lazy, and the warmth of it wrapped around her like a hug.

"Aye, I'm late already. I must check on your father and see to the chores."

"We have a servant for the outside work."

"Then I have breakfast to prepare. I can't believe your brothers would think well of me if I let them starve."

"My brothers know how to fend for themselves." Jonah sat up in bed, the sheets gliding down his body to rest dangerously low at his hips. Dark hair gathered there and drew her gaze. "Are you remembering last night? Remembering how you liked it?"

"You are a devil, you are. I was right about you all along." Heat stained her face at the remembered images hardly decent in the light of day, or even in the first scattering of daylight

A brow quirked. "I'm too big to push into a mud puddle, as you did when we were children and I pulled your braid."

"Aye, but not so big that I can't shove you out of that bed."

" 'Tis because you want to see me naked and aroused. I can oblige." He rolled back the covers, revealing bronzed skin and powerfully built man and a jutting hardness that he seemed so proud of. "Forget the chores. Forget breakfast. I want you, Tessa."

"Goodness. 'Tis after six o'clock in the morning. 'Tis not decent."

"And was it decent last night?" He unfolded his big body full length. "You were more than eager in the dark. Let us see how wild you can be in the daylight."

"Go ahead and tempt me. 'Twill not work." In truth, her blood nearly boiled in her veins at the sight of him. Why did it have to be him? She had always prayed to find a nice man, a quiet one, maybe bookish, decent, and kind. But not one of those words could be used to describe this man towering before her, brash and bold and *naked*.

So very naked. She could hardly ignore that thick stiff length of him, staring right at her. Her knees felt shaky. And her entire body melted.

"Admit it, Tessa. You want me." His bare feet padded on the wood floor. How close he was. She took a step backward. " 'Tis there in your eyes, as dark as desire. You enjoyed making love last night"

" 'Twas not too terrible," she admitted. And lied boldly. Terrible? 'Twas indescribably heavenly. "But already the day has begun and we can't lie about when there's work to be done."

"There will be time enough for work." A slow grin stretched his mouth at one corner as he wrapped both hands around her wrists, holding her captive. "Come, back to bed with me. I'll let you be on top."

"*On top?*" Humor and a devil's light sparkled in his eyes, so deep and rich she could lose herself in them. "You're naught but a rogue, a wicked man through and through."

"Guilty as charged." A dimple etched into his cheek. He was enjoying this too much.

"See? You admit it. You were entirely responsible for my behavior last night"

"Me?" He crooked one brow, "*I* was responsible?"

"Aye, you. A proper wife lies there dutifully, but you, you made me—"

"A proper wife? Oh, that's a stretch of the truth. From our first kiss you were a wicked enchantress with that fiery mouth of yours, and in the forest, offering me your breasts the way you did—"

"Offering you? You did as you pleased."

"And you moaned the entire time. Just like last night." His lips grazed her knuckles, and his tongue flicked out to lave the sensitive skin of her inner wrist. "Come, let me make you moan again."

"A decent husband would not know how to make a woman moan like that."

Dark eyes snapped, crackling like fire in a hearth, intense, dangerous. "I never said I was a decent man. Or husband. I know how much you liked it, Tessa. And how much you are tempted now. Your eyes are naught but black, your breath comes fast and light in your chest, and your pulse skips beneath my touch. Admit it"

"I can plainly see how tempted you are." She tried to joke, but there was nothing humorous in his rock-hard shaft, or in the desire plain and naked in his eyes, and all for her. "But your brothers will think—"

" 'Tis none of their business what I do with my wife."

His mouth claimed hers in a storm of heat and fire. Like a flame, she felt burned by him. Burned by a fast crackling want that snapped through her veins and sizzled in her very bones.

He backed her up against the wall until there was no space between them. She could feel the hard wall of his chest against her breasts, the steely bunch of his thighs fitted between hers, and his rock-hard shaft slanted against the curve of her stomach.

"You're not responding like a proper wife." He broke their kiss only to tug at her buttons.

" 'Tis hard to be proper with a man as wicked as you." Her breath came fast and light. Her whole body felt aflame, ready to be engulfed by this sharp pounding need for him.

"So you blame me again?" he chuckled, rich and liquid warm as he dipped his head to draw her bared breast into his mouth.

"Aye. 'Tis all your fault." Such thrilling pleasure. Tessa tipped her head back to rest against the wall, her eyes drifting shut. The sweet pressure of his mouth on her nipple drew taut a band of sensation low in her abdomen. Tingly and heavy and incredible, she was ready to surrender to him even in the light of day and let him strip off her clothes and make love to her until this heady need for him was sated.

A knock tapped at the closed door. "Jonah?"

"Not now, Andy," Jonah growled out, lifting his head from her breasts. "I'm busy."

"But 'Tis Father."

Jonah squeezed his eyes shut, the muscles standing out in his strong jaw and the column of his neck.

"I must go." She pressed a kiss to Jonah's stubbled jaw, rough and so wondrously male. "You can be wicked later, mayhap at nighttime when it's much more decent"

"Decency be damned." His gaze clamped on her, intense and intimate, sparkling with a knowledge of what was to come.

Her heart skipped three beats, for she wanted to be held in his arms, pinned beneath him, and feel that spiraling pleasure only he could give her.

She hadn't known married life would be so wondrous. Mother had spoken of the pleasure of the marriage bed but only indirectly.

Tessa fastened her buttons, and Jonah stepped away. Still

naked, still aroused, still wanting her, but sadness now snapped in his eyes and tightened the muscles of his jaw.

"Go to him. I'll get dressed and come help you."

" 'Twill be interesting to see how your breeches fit," she could not help teasing.

Imagine, her, Tessa Bradford, teasing. Never in her life had she felt this happy. And it was only one day, less than twenty-four hours of being Jonah's bride.

'Twas a very fine thing to be.

Jonah pushed open the door to Father's chamber. New candles burned on the stand by the bed, where the weak old man coughed fitfully. The hacking painful sound filled the room and the empty chambers of his cold dark heart.

"Yesterday was too exciting for him." Tessa looked up when he entered the room. Her long hair was brushed but not yet tied back, caressing the delicate cut of her cheekbones and jaw, softening her features, rendering her beautiful.

If Tessa had worn her hair down and smiled just once, likely half the men in the village would have dropped to their knees before her. Even he had been guilty in seeing the worst in her, in this woman who had cared so dutifully for an ill and dying mother, as he had not done for his own father.

Aye, she was a woman of courage and strength, of more goodness and beauty than anyone he knew. Even now, she tended Father with tender hands, angelic hands, smoothing a cloth over the old man's wrinkled brow.

"I can't seem to catch air," Father wheezed between dry, chest-deep coughs.

"I told you to take care, not to become overtired. You refused to listen, so don't expect any sympathy from me." But the soft curve of her mouth gentled the words and the caring in her eyes, how mesmerizing it was.

"Jonah, will you bring me some boiling water? I would do it myself, but I don't want to leave him."

He could only nod, his throat tight. Tight with fear for his father who appeared to be scarcely breathing. Tight with gratefulness for Tessa, who did not shirk her duty.

"I'll bring up your breakfast as well." He resisted the urge to kiss her, to thank her for what she had done. This was all the proof he needed. He had made the right choice in marrying her.

He left with the image of her sitting at Father's side, candlelight sheening the ebony beauty of her hair. He tapped down the stairs, glad at least this worry he carried was groundless. Marriage might not prove to be so horrible after all.

"Quite a grin you're wearing, brother." Thomas looked up from the hearth.

"Aye, 'Tis amazing you are in such good humor." Andy sat at the table, his plate heaped with baked goods.

"Look how at ease he is. I bet our sharp-tongued Mistress Tessa is not always so severe." Thomas scooped fried eggs from a sizzling skillet. "Comes as quite a surprise to me, but looks can be deceiving, eh, Jonah?"

"More than you know." He grabbed an extra plate from the cupboard. "Is that kettle boiling yet?"

" 'Tis done. I just set it off the heat." Thomas set the platter of food on the table. "How is Father?"

"His cough did not sound good." Jonah filled a plate for Tessa. He didn't know what she liked, so he chose both ham and sausages to go with the eggs. And a slice of pumpkin bread and a piece of tasty looking streusel. "I don't want you gluttons eating all the food whilst I'm gone."

"If you walk away, you're taking your chances," Andy teased with a mouthful of streusel.

"Strike me dead," Thomas roared. "I cannot believe our fearless hero of a brother is fixing a plate for his wife."

"Aye, look how tenderly he set the sausages next to the egg."

"Mayhap he is in love."

"Enough," Jonah commanded. "Love has naught to do with it. Tessa is tending Father. She cannot care for him on an empty stomach."

"See how he blushes?" Andy piped up. " 'Tis lust then."

"Lust is a safer emotion than love, my brother." Jonah swiped a glass of cider from the table. "Andy, you're eating all the sausages. Come with me and fetch the kettle from the hearth. Tessa needs hot water."

"What I can't believe is that you seem satisfied with the match." Thomas stood and handed Andy a hot pad. "Jonah, I know you married her for Father."

"Aye, and right now she is at his side. 'Tis a good match, brother. Try not to scare her with that ugly face of yours when you see her next."

"Too late," Andy quipped. " 'Tis why she thinks you so handsome, Jonah. Poor Tessa looked at Thomas first and even you looked good in comparison."

"How is he?" Tessa wrung the last bit of herbed water from the basin. "Resting now. He feels warm, but the fever has not returned, at least not yet. I fear it may."

Jonah knelt beside her, both strong hands resting on his knees. "I want him to recover."

"As do I." She saw the worry in his eyes, dark with fear. "You know I will do all I can, for he is my father now, too."

His throat worked. "Aye, that he is. No one could tend him as well, Tessa. Or do so much. I'll always be grateful."

"As will I." The morning had stretched away, a weary time of worry and work, for she feared the worst. If the colonel worsened, then he was far too weak to fight another bout of fever. And yet, Jonah had been there, bringing her breakfast, fetching water and wood, letting her know she was so valued.

She'd tended many ill in this village over the years and had mostly been an outsider intruding into a family's circle, seeing their innermost struggles and problems. Now, for the first time, she belonged.

And all because of Jonah.

"A ship is in at the docks." He reached up and brushed a straggle of hair from her eyes, such a tender gesture. One of a loving husband for a wife. "I know Father is ill, but you have been here since dawn. Mayhap you want to go down and see what they have for sale."

"There's nothing I need more than to take care of your father." It touched her, that he would offer her this. "He could worsen at any minute. Besides, another ship may dock tomorrow. Or next week. I have all I need."

"But we're without a house servant and there may be some on board. I think you should decide if there is anyone suitable, as you will be overseeing her."

"But there is not much to do here. Surely I can—"

"Nay, Tessa." He laid his hand on her shoulder, and his touch sizzled. "I didn't bring you here to work like a servant for us. I'm not like your grandfather, and I will always despise that man for how he treated you. You are my wife now, and you need not work for a roof over your head."

"Oh, Jonah." He truly cared for her, just as he'd said. He loved her, it was written in the gleam of emotion in his eyes, in the gentle bass of his voice. His touches claimed her, and she remembered how he'd treasured her in their chamber last night. How he drove her to such surrender, to sure, unbearable pleasure. Only love could do that.

"Andy and Thomas will stay. Father is resting well now. He will likely do so for a few more hours."

"But I'm not so sure—"

"A new servant is necessary. You've seen how my brothers and I live. Pigs are less slovenly."

"Aye, I had that thought myself." How his kindness made her chest ache, made her heart hurt sweetly.

"See? You'll be saving us, for if cleanliness is next to godliness, we are in deep danger of losing our souls."

"That's been my opinion for a long time." Barely able to restrain her smile, Tessa laid the rag to rest in the basin. "I guess duty calls. I'll find a servant and hope 'Tis enough to redeem you."

"You are an angel." Laughing, he stood and held out his hand. His big strong hand that engulfed hers so easily with the thrilling texture of his male-rough skin.

After leaving careful instructions with both Thomas and Andy and after agreeing to wear the cloak Jonah had given her, Tessa stepped out into the weak sunshine with her hand on her husband's strong arm.

The village was not that far of a ride, and the wharf with the wide gray river lay just beyond. Many walked along the common road, and Tessa felt their gazes as Jonah guided the small wagon past.

"Looks as if news travels fast." He leaned close.

She shivered as his shoulder brushed hers and stayed there. A small connection, but it made her feel stronger. "Aye, there was much speculation when it was learned you were returning to Baybrooke to marry, as your father requested."

"I'm surprised anyone would even remember me, I had been gone so long."

"You're the eldest son of the colonel, so respected in this

town." Tessa's chest tightened. "And there were many who thought they had a good chance of being your bride."

"I bet many didn't think that I would choose you." He smiled then, one that was a blend of warmth and bedevilment all at once. "I am an unpredictable fellow."

"You take pride in that, I see." How good he made her feel inside, in her heart that had been lonely for love. "You married me because my grandfather thought I was compromised."

"I didn't have to marry you." His eyes darkened, and some of the teasing ebbed from his eyes, like sunlight behind leaden clouds. "Your grandfather still wanted you to marry Horace Walling. I had to pay both men handsomely to convince them otherwise."

"Usually the bride brings something to the marriage."

"I do not want a dowry, Tessa. You're prize enough."

He valued her that much. She felt her throat fill and stared hard at her mittened hands. Tears burned beneath her eyes, tears of such great happiness. Who had thought all those years horrible Jonah Hunter had teased her in dame school, then ignored her as they both grew to adulthood, he had harbored these feelings so strong, he had married her, wanted her above all others. He valued her, thought her a prize.

No one, not even her beloved mother, had said those words, made her feel so special. The warmth in her chest grew, expanding beneath her ribs so that it burned in the hollow of her throat, beneath the spot where her collarbones met and her pulse beat fast and fluttery.

"You've done so much for Father." He took her hand in his and only then did she realize they were at the river.

Villagers crowded the wooden dock, faint sunlight glinted on dark water, and a ship with three furled sails waited patiently for the next breath of wind.

"Come, let's see if there is a servant here who will suit you."

The din of the crowd nearly silenced as Jonah lifted her from the wagon. She could have climbed down herself, but she didn't want to miss any opportunity to feel his touch, even here in a public place where so many eyes watched and wondered.

"It seems to me we ought to look at the fabric, too." He took her hand, and his touch never left her as he led her through the staring crowd.

So many of the people she knew and many she'd tended when

they were ill stood gaping at her. Or turned to whisper to one another—the Sandersons who had lost their aged aunt early this winter, the Carpenters, whose daughter nearly died when the strange fever had swept through the village last year, and more, so many more.

"Major Hunter, welcome home to Baybrooke." The innkeeper, Bernard Sawyer, extended his hand.

"Bernard, 'Tis been a long while. Still serving that swill you call ale?"

"Aye, that I am." The ruddy-faced man tipped his hat to her. "Congratulations, Mistress Hunter, on your recent wedding."

"Thank you." Strange it was, to be greeted as Jonah's bride. And yet she was proud to stand beside so handsome a man, who treated others with respect. Some people in the village believed themselves to be finer than others because they had more money and wore better clothes, but not Jonah.

"Look, the captain has spread out his yard goods on that board table." Jonah, taller than she was, could see more easily through the crowd. "Now, no protests allowed. I want to see my wife in something other than dreary colors. Go ahead, pick out what you like. I'll go see what kind of servants are aboard ship."

Jonah squeezed her hand before he left. Her heart thudding, she watched him weave through the milling crowd, his gait steady and determined, his shoulders broad, especially when compared to so many other men's. Today his dark hair was swept back and tied at his nape, and an unruly shock tumbled over his brow. She saw him in profile speaking to the ship's captain.

"He doesn't love you, you know."

"Violet." Tessa spun around. She'd been so intent on watching Jonah she hadn't noticed anything else.

"Everyone is saying it. He would have married me if you hadn't tricked him." Violet's mouth twisted into an ugly sneer that seemed to drain all the natural beauty from her face. "I was the one he came to see after morning meeting that Sunday. Me. Not a sour-faced old maid who had to act like a harlot to snare a man's last name."

"She's right." Charity sauntered up behind her daughter, mouth pursed, eyes hard. "You ought to be ashamed to show your face among decent people. I have had Ely speak with the selectmen of the village. While you were working your wiles on poor Major

Hunter, you were breaking curfew. Not to mention acting lasciviously. There are penalties for that."

Tessa clamped her mouth shut. Horrible, unspeakable words burned on her tongue. Her hands fisted into tight balls of anger. She had endured Charity's cruel tongue and mean spirit for far too many years, and she would not do so any longer. She itched to speak her peace, for once, without the threat of being kicked out into the street, but she could not. She would not embarrass Jonah that way, or herself, by losing her temper.

"Excuse me, Charity."

"You're not going anywhere until I've had my say." The woman darted around her daughter, face set, marching like a soldier to the front line. "You have been the bane of my existence for the last ten years. You shoved your way into my house with that weak mother of yours—"

"Don't say one word against my mother," Tessa hissed, careful to keep her voice low. "You have no right, you who have not lifted a hand to perform a single domestic task for most of those ten years. I chopped the wood and I made the meals and I did the laundry and I made soap and candles and thread for the weaving. So not one word, Charity."

"You are likely to be no better than your silly mother, a foolish weak-willed simpleton who could not see the man she married had a use for her. Not love, a use for her."

" 'Tis enough, Mistress Bradford." Low that voice, rumbling like thunder over a valley, sure and strong and laced with warning. "I could hear your accusations all the way to the water's edge. And I assure you, I never set my sights on your shallow daughter. I married Tessa by choice. Anyone who says differently will answer to me."

Charity shrank at Jonah's quiet, controlled anger. The crowd silenced, all eyes turning toward them, waiting for what was to come next. Violet's face puckered into tears.

Tessa stepped forward. "Jonah, 'Tis all right. Vicious words cannot do much harm."

"You're wrong, but I will not argue." He took her hand, his touch reassuring.

Her heart soared, and the warmth in her chest deepened. Her affection for Jonah grew steadily brighter with each breath and with every beat of her heart.

CHAPTER ELEVEN

"Andy, do not stare at Anya." Tessa halted behind Andy's chair at the table and whispered low, so the slender young woman heating wash water at the hearth could not hear. "She is uncertain enough about a new situation, so it would be best for her not to have a man drooling from his chin every time she walks by."

"I do not drool!" Andy snapped his jaw shut, teeth clacking.

Jonah could see more denial on his brother's face, but the young man held it back, still afraid enough of Tessa. "Andy, I saw a drop drip off your chin. My advice is to swallow now and then."

"Aye, 'Tis advice you should heed." Thomas struggled not to laugh as he stood from the table. "Tessa, is Father awake?"

"I just left him and he's sleeping. Fitfully. Mayhap he would rest easier with one of his sons at his side." Her gaze landed on Jonah.

He felt the uncomfortable accusation. "I will go, Thomas. Stay and keep an eye on Andy." He lowered his voice. "I would hate to have that poor girl slip in a puddle of drool."

"Jonah, 'Tis not funny. I have not teased you about drooling after your wife." Andy stood, hands balled tight.

He laughed. "Aye, we can drool together. Sit down and ask her for a cup of tea."

"I had best act as chaperone," Thomas observed quietly. "Tessa, you could have chosen an ugly old woman. There would be less complications."

"She was the one I liked." Tessa smiled at Thomas as she swept on by, a beautiful smile that Jonah suspected until now, only he had seen.

Jonah watched surprise mark Thomas' face. One dark brow quirked. His Tessa was beautiful. Fatigue bruised the delicate skin beneath her eyes, but the years of hardship and strain had vanished, replaced by a beauty that was more than skin deep.

He watched as she poured steaming water into a basin, her movements efficient and swift, but graceful, too. Her dark hair tumbled over her shoulder as she spoke low to the new indentured servant, a young woman, still practically a girl, without family, who had, he suspected by the sorrow in her dark eyes, been sold to the ship's captain somewhere along the way, mayhap illegally. It happened often enough.

He did not question his wife's choice. Mayhap she saw something he did not in the plain, pale-faced girl who would not look up and meet anyone's gaze. Anya worked hard, already he could see proof of that, and the meal she had cooked so that Tessa could remain with Father was some of the best food he'd had in many years.

Tessa led the way up the stairs. He could not lift his gaze from the sway of her rump beneath her dark skirts. His groin still ached with the need they'd built up early this morning. He wanted her more than air to breathe.

"Thank you for insisting I needed help around here. 'Twas thoughtful of you, for I've always been the one doing all the work alone. 'Twill be good to have someone to share it with."

His conscience twinged. He had bought the servant so Tessa could devote more time to Father. But he was glad, she was pleased. When she twisted around to smile at him, her eyes glittered with happiness, unveiled and bright. 'Twas the same way she'd looked when he'd prodded her into choosing several lengths of new fabric.

"I never thanked you for what you did today."

"For what? Pushing you up against the bedchamber wall and working my way beneath your gown?" Teasing was easier than facing the emotions beneath.

"You're an incorrigible man. I was referring to the way you handled Charity. How you stood up to her. No one has ever done that for me. Ever."

"I only spoke the truth, Tessa." He fought the tug of deeper emotions, of ways he had not let himself feel for so long. "I never had my eye set on Violet Bradford. I'd have run screaming all the way to Boston rather than wed a cold-hearted chit like her."

A small, satisfied smile touched her mouth, a smile he wanted to kiss until she melted against him. "Thomas will watch over Father tonight. Mayhap we can head to bed a little early."

"Nay, I need to keep watch on Samuel." She used Father's proper name with quiet affection, as gentle as dawn. "He appears to be doing a bit better, but I'm leery. I know in my heart I need to watch carefully for any sign of the fever returning."

Half aroused already, he gritted his teeth against the building desire for her expanding in his breeches. He'd been thinking of little else all day, of stripping her in his bed and feasting on the sweetness of her breasts, of listening to the growing urgency in her moans, of her restless body rising up to mate with his.

But Father was the reason why he'd married her in the first place. So the old man would have the care he deserved in these last days of his life.

He sighed, resigned to a night without passion. There would be time enough for making love. Tessa strode down the corridor and into Father's room, her skirts swishing, and beneath them, the tantalizing sway of her hips and thighs.

The old man looked up from his pillows, and laughter crinkled in knowledgeable eyes. "You look like a hungry wolf, son. Don't suppose 'Tis something you can tell your father about?"

"Nay, and you well know it."

Jonah watched Tessa set the basin on the night table, her movements lithe and graceful. The brush of her fingers to the water's steaming surface reminded him of her feather-light touch across his chest. The twist of her mouth into a smile made him taste again the heat of her kisses. The flicker of her gaze to his reminded him of their joining, when she stared up at him from between heavily lidded eyes.

"I left you sleeping." She settled down at the bedside, her face tender.

"Aye, I awakened to find my angel of mercy had left me."

"I needed more water. I could fetch you some broth."

"Nay. I have a craving for real food and you'll not let me have it." Father's hand, strong and straight even with age, caught Tessa's. "It did me good to see you and my boy married. To think he harbored a fondness for you all these years. I well remember him as a little schoolboy racing home many afternoons complaining of his muddy breeches and blaming sweet little you."

"I shoved him, all right." She laughed. "Trust me, he deserved it."

"Little boys always do." He winked, a weak smile coming to light his face. How his eyes twinkled. "Now my son is giving you a different kind of tumble, and he pleases you, judging by the color in your cheeks."

" 'Tis only because of the steam from the boiling water."

"Say what you will, but an old man can recognize these things." Father sighed, his smile weak and pale, but lingering.

"You look better." Jonah circled the bed to draw another chair to the edge of the mattress. "You had us worried for a while there."

"I cannot deny it. I fear my time is near." Father sighed, a sadness plucking at the papery wrinkles at his eyes. "I'm well contented to see you sensibly married. Tessa, I think that foul tea is bewitching me."

" 'Tis possible. I said a spell while steeping it." A soft humor twinkled in her compassionate eyes. "Now go to sleep, and stop fighting it. Trust me, you'll feel better come morning."

"Aye, or I'll be dead. Either way, 'twill be a change." Chuckling, then coughing, Father relaxed into the pillows. "Make yourself useful and read to me, boy."

"I already have the book in hand." Jonah leafed through the pages, remembering where he'd left off.

Tessa's gaze snared his. The warm glow of candlelight caressed her face and illuminated the sweet blue of her eyes. And resonated with the hues of her heart—gentle, kind, and infinitely caring.

Not the heart of a sensible old maid after all. He thought of Charity Bradford's cruel words today at the wharf, and how crushed Tessa had been without the hard armor she'd built over the years, the sharp-tongued spinster who could handle any insult or any situation.

He saw for the first time what a grave mistake he'd made, assuming she had a heart as lost to love as his, lost from too much pain and too many dark nights without comfort or hope or dreams.

He bowed his head and began reading, the meter and imagery of the poem rolling off his tongue, but never touching his heart.

"You mean so much to him." Tessa felt the candlelight glint in her eyes, saw how it softened the hard chiseled angles of Jonah's jaw and the strong blade of his nose.

His well-shaped hands cradled the open book, as if he treasured the words there. "I'm his eldest son. Such high expectations he set for me."

" 'Tis why he's so proud, no doubt."

"Proud?" Jonah shook his head in disbelief and closed the volume. "He sleeps now."

"Aye, he fought the sleeping powder I made him. He has been sleeping, but not well. As I said, 'Tis best for him that you're here. He seems brighter, more determined."

"If this is truly his time, there's naught either of us can do to stop it."

"Aye, I've seen it often enough." Tessa stood and reached to the low shelf over the bed. Her fingers grasped three fresh candles. "Some who seem strong enough to fight die, whilst others who are more ill survive. Sometimes I think it has to do with the will to stay with loved ones. I've not given up hope on your father."

"Truly?" How deep his eyes, filled with an abiding affection.

"Truly. He has you." *And so do I.* She held those words back, although they lived deep inside, in a place that had not known love in too long.

"You place too much importance on me."

"On strong, heroic Major Hunter?" She now believed him to be.

"Trust me, I'm not so heroic." He bowed his head.

Tessa lit a new taper with the stub of a dying one. " 'Tis all your father talked about, how you received this commission or that, another promotion, or won a greater victory. You made him proud, Jonah. Everyone in this village knows it."

He said nothing, but sat in silence as the candlelight brushed at his shoulders and the edges of his face, as the clock ticked and wood smoke puffed into the room with a gust of wind. "I'm but an ordinary man, Tessa. With ordinary flaws and failures."

"I never said you weren't flawed." She set the last lit candle into its holder.

"So I have you to remind me, lest I get too big of a head from listening to such high praise." It hurt to smile, it hurt to feel.

And yet she touched his heart in ways he could not explain. How she moved, the way she smiled, the steady quiet strength of her. She did not seem afraid of death, not afraid to touch it, to breathe it, to feel its cold shadows creeping from the corners of the room toward the light.

"Let me guess. You didn't like the army." She knelt at his side, bringing with her the sweet scent of roses and the herbs she'd last steeped for Father's tea. Her hands, not silken and soft as many of those silly young women's in the village, were slightly rough and reddened, but were beautiful just the same. And the touch of her heated skin to his moved him like nothing else.

"Nay. I was just a small boy fed on my father's tales of his time in the army, and I loved him."

"You wanted to be just like him."

"Aye." He didn't like how Tessa's sharp gaze could look inside and see his thoughts, his truths. "I left home a man determined to do my father proud and protect this land from marauding Indians and the French."

"I can't believe there is much pride in war."

"Why do you say that? Others think—"

"I have seen far too much dying. I can't think 'twould be easy to inflict such suffering, to become a killer."

"You see into my soul, then."

Her eyes shadowed. "Nay, just into your eyes."

Relieved, he was glad she could not see the darkness there, for every life he had taken in battle and for every life he saved. He'd not expected brutality, and the burden of it still weighed on his shoulders. "He was an Indian brave, no older than I."

"Who was?"

"The first man I killed." He did not want to tell her this, did not want her to see the flaws so deep. "My first battle."

"You remember?" How dark her eyes, full of sympathy, of unspoken questions. But not judgment. Nay, that would come in time.

"I've never forgotten." His throat closed tight on the truths he kept silent for ten long years. "He was like me, fighting for what he believed in. I had the luck to dodge his arrow meant for my heart.

'Twas naught but luck. I slashed and killed him in one swift act. I will never forget his face, never forget what I saw there."

"What?"

His chest squeezed when her fingers curled around his. "That he was like me and no different. He probably had a father who loved him, and younger brothers at home who would miss him. His life was gone, spent on the muddy field that day. *That* is battle. I've not been the same since or held the same beliefs over what is right and what is wrong."

"You're not so bad of a man as you think." Her mouth brushed his, gentle and comforting, like sunlight after winter, bright and earnest and full of hope.

Hope. If Tessa could see the good in him, mayhap there was some after all.

* * *

His throat scratchy from reading aloud for hours without stop, Jonah reached for a glass of water. Father slept, breathing unevenly, a rattle clearly audible with each exhaled breath.

The water was cool, for he was on the far side of the bed and the fire didn't warm this side of the room, the north side where a night wind chilled the wall and window.

"Tessa?"

She didn't stir. She sat straight up in the wooden chair, her back resting heavily on the wooden spires. Her chin tilted forward, and her rich mane of dark curls hid her face from his sight.

So, she slept. The clock chimed the hour—three in the morning. He remembered the long nights without relief caring for Father, and then their wedding night when he'd loved her thoroughly and late, and there had been little sleep. How tired she must be, and his heart cinched tight.

Father slept, and he could always awaken her if the old man worsened. Jonah set aside the volume of poetry and circled the bed.

How still she looked in sleep. 'Twas an intimate thing, to watch her like this. Her body relaxed, her hands curled loosely in her lap, her breathing light and steady. How soft her face was in this light, surely not the face of a spinster his age, feared by the entire village.

Indeed, today on the docks, many a man had wished him luck with such a bride, mayhap believing he'd been forced to marry for having a little bit of sport, as men were wont to do.

And he had done his best to straighten out that misconception. He didn't want anyone to think ill of this woman he had taken to wife. She had a courage and a strength he'd never dreamed of having, the patient honor it took to care for the dying and the living. She in her own way had probably saved more lives and made a better mark on the world.

There were many kinds of heroism, many different brands of courage.

He lifted her gently, gathering her slight weight into his arms. Her head nestled beneath his chin, her sweet woman's body settled against his chest. He carried her to bed, slipped off her shoes and dress, and tucked the quilt up to her chin.

She did not move, not even to nestle into the pillows. She slept as still as an angel and to him looked twice as beautiful.

A velvet warmth pressed against her throat. Tessa felt the deliciously soft mattress beneath her, saw the pink luminous glow at the window, inhaled the wood smoke and bayberry clinging to her husband's skin. Her husband who was nibbling hot wet kisses across the back of her neck. She lay on her side, and he was spooned around her, his body hard and cradled against hers.

"Good morning." His words swept across the damp skin he'd been licking.

Tessa sighed. "I'm supposed to be tending Samuel."

"And what about your husband?" His hand circled around her ribs and covered her breast. "I need tending, too."

"You're not ill."

"Nay, 'Tis a different malady I suffer from." His fingers kneaded and molded her sensitive flesh. "Mayhap I can ask you to tend me."

"I don't think there's a cure for your suffering." Tessa could not hold back the bubble of happiness in her chest, expanding with every breath, with every press of his lips to the hollow between her shoulder blades.

"You can feel how swollen I've become."

"Aye, something is very hard against the back of my thigh." Tessa rolled over to face him. His smile became their kiss, molten and tingling and demanding. "Mayhap I could soak that part of you in ice. 'Twill probably take down the swelling."

" 'Twould work, I'm sure, but I had something else in mind."

His chuckle vibrated through her.

"I know exactly what you want, but 'Tis already dawn and what about your father? I don't even remember leaving him last night."

"Because I carried you here."

"You did?" Maybe she had always thought Jonah Hunter handsome. And maybe all this time she'd held a secret liking for him. But now as his wife and knowing him like this, every time he stood up for her, took care of her, told her how special she was, why it made that affection inside her heart grow until it was so bright she couldn't see anything else.

"Father is better. He's already been bellowing for something to eat besides your thin broth and bird-dropping tea."

"That tea is made from a mixture of herbs." She laughed. "If he is complaining, then he's on the mend."

"Aye, and we may have some time alone. After all, I have this swollen part of me and I hear you are an excellent healer."

"Not even I can heal your wickedness, Jonah. In fact, I have reason to believe 'Tis terribly catching."

"My wickedness?"

"Aye." She splayed her hands on his chest, so solid, so broad, and delighted in the male-texture of bronzed skin and downy hair. "For I've been feeling very wicked lately."

"Have you been experiencing any swelling?"

Laughter spiraled deep inside, where happiness and a building ache for this man filled her. " 'Tis possible. Mayhap I have need of your ministrations."

"I'm no healer, but I possess a few skills of my own." His lips wrapped around her left nipple.

Sharp pleasure sliced through her. Her head lulled back. Already she felt wet and restless, wanting him. "What skills you have."

"Aye. Seems to have had some effect here, at your nipple."

"I can feel it." She sighed when he suckled this time, drawing her deep into his mouth, and then arched her back. "And even lower."

"Truly? Mayhap I should see for myself."

His hands caressed dazzling trails of heat down her ribs, over her abdomen and ever lower, to that private place that pulsed and ached for more than his touch. His clever fingers found her fiery center and stroked. Bright white pleasure jolted through her.

"I see what you mean. I think I can cure this problem." His

fingers grazed the sensitive inner folds and circled once, then again. She moaned low at the hot sensation that built there. Then he reached up and wrapped his arms around her, holding her tight, and they rolled together until she was on top gazing down into the dark sparkles of his eyes.

"Lucky you are that I happened along." His hands settled on her hips.

She felt the hard ridge of his shaft thrumming against her stomach. All thought fled. Only feeling remained. He gazed up at her with tenderness, with such adoration it frightened her, made her wish for endless nights to fill with this wondrous closeness.

"I want you." His hands lifted her, and she rose over him. "So very much."

"As I want you." Her breath caught when his shaft nudged the sensitive curve of her inner thighs. She opened to him, drawing him in with one smooth glide.

"We're good together, eh?" How dark his eyes were. How low his voice. "I can't believe my luck in having you for my wife."

"Jonah." He felt so good inside her, thick and pulsing, stretching her tight. Her entire body responded, drawing taut around him. Emotion as bright as a springtime sun, as full as a blue moon, shone inside her, growing more sure every time they rocked together.

His hands on her hips guided her. She sat up, and the change of position shifted the feel of his shaft within her.

Such a thrilling feeling. She gazed down at him, melting at the way he looked up at her, as if she were beautiful, truly beautiful.

And he made her feel that way. Overcome, she moved in a slow rhythm, just to watch his jaw strum tight as she tortured him. But he stroked more deeply inside her with every slow thrust, and she was the one tortured. Control tumbled away. Heat stretched tight in her abdomen and built hot and fast there, where they joined. Soon he was bucking up to meet her strokes, driving her toward aching, unending sensation.

Surrender came in a series of wrenching ripples of muscle and soul. Tears burned her eyes as sharp pleasure exploded, tearing through her over and over again. Sharp, searing, so thrilling she could not bear it. So brilliant there was only sensation, only the two of them lost and burning.

She felt his climax, the tensed agony as he cried out, the rush of heat as he spilled his seed. His arms banded around her and pulled her tight against his chest. She held him, feeling as if she could never let him go. No one had ever moved her this much, made her feel cherished and wanted and more valued than any riches.

"I love you, Jonah," she breathed, content to hold him for the rest of her life.

CHAPTER TWELVE

"'Tis almost time to begin turning the earth. The ground is nearly thawed." Thomas kicked at a clod of dirt in the fallow fields, sodden from melting snow and ice.

Rain drummed to the ground in streaks of bleak dreary gray. The world was naught but bare-limbed trees and charcoal sky and dark earth. 'Twas the time between winter and spring, when the grasses had not yet awakened, when the earth itself still slept. A few sparrows startled, flying up to perch on low boughs.

Jonah tipped the rainwater off the brim of his hat.

"You're no farmer, Thomas. I'm afraid to listen to you."

"Aye, you should be. Andy is the one with the experience, since he stayed home longer than any of us." Thomas stared off toward the river, where a ship struggled to fill those pristine white sails with a breath of wind to take them on their way.

"Where is he? Chasing the young Anya's skirts?"

"Tessa told him that she'd have his head for that, and he believed her." Thomas chuckled, rubbing the back of his neck with one hand. "I think Tessa is happy with us, with you."

"Even living with men like us has to be a far sight better than enduring Charity Bradford's tongue lashings."

"Aye. Andy and I discussed it just this morning. 'Tis the first time either one of us has actually seen the infamous spinster smile."

"She's no longer a spinster."

"Many think you and she were having liaisons all this time. Her grandfather refused to swear to her whereabouts at night. I think he likes maliciously spreading gossip."

"Then I'll need to put a stop to it" Troubled, Jonah thought of the work ahead of him, both in his marriage and here, tilling these lands. "Father is alive because of her."

"Have you given any thought about how she feels?"

"What thought?" Jonah knew where this conversation was headed, and he spun around, walking fast toward the riverbank. High from snowmelt, the Connecticut swept past as leaden as the sky above. "Where's Andy? He's supposed to join us."

"He complained of a headache and asked Tessa for a cure. She steeped tree bark and told him to drink it."

"Did he fear she might poison him?" Jonah laughed at the image of his brother, cocksure on the outside, but not so on the inside.

"He said it tasted foul, but he drank it all." Thomas braced his hands on his hips and studied the river, silent and deep. "You married Tessa to help Father, and 'twas the only reason. What will you do if she falls in love with you? Will you love her in return?"

His chest tightened. Tessa's confession in his arms still haunted him days later. "I treat her well. I respect her."

" 'Tis not the same and you know it. Women are different from us. They want romance and pretty words."

"I have no pretty words, and Tessa knows that. 'Tis the reason I didn't want to marry a young girl who knew little of the real world. Tessa does. Her life has been hard, and I've done what I can to make it better. This afternoon I have decided to take her to a seamstress for new dresses."

"I'm not arguing over how well you treat her, brother." Thomas reached over the fence to give the lumbering cow, heavy with calf, a rub on her nose. "Anyone can see how happy she is. She hums, she smiles, she is pleasant. 'Tis like a different woman. Does she believe you love her?"

"I may have given her that impression." Jonah knelt to study the cow's underbelly. Her udder was not full or dripping. The birth would not be immediate. "We'll need to bring this cow into the stable before she calves."

"But Tessa—"

"Don't worry about my wife, Thomas. We both know what love can do to a man, and no woman will have that kind of power over me. I like Tessa well enough, mayhap even more, but I'll never love her. She will never have me on my knees, doing her will just to see a glimpse of her smile."

"Ah, we both remember how our stepmother used Father. And the ruin that came from it. But I've been thinking. Mayhap not all women are made of the same cloth. Tessa works alongside the servant, not lording power over her. She has asked for little and puts you and Father above her own needs. I think because she expects affection from you in return."

"And why are you worrying about my wife?" Jonah ground out.

"Because she gazes after you with puppy dog eyes. As if you are her own personal hero who saved her from a brutal marriage to Horace Walling or a life of servitude in her grandfather's home. She lights up when you smile at her in a way I have never seen."

I love you, Jonah. How her breathy, honest words haunted his memory, rang in the empty chambers of his heart.

Love was an emotion, if genuine, that came from within. His heart had been numbed from years of battle so that, like ground frozen too long, nothing could grow from it. No matter how bright the sun or how temperate the spring.

The village of Baybrooke stretched out before her, the commons a dull winter-grass green beneath a sky as gray as regret.

Jonah set his strong hands on her waist and lifted her down from the wagon. She rather liked the feeling of being in his arms, even just for a moment, the bunch of his muscled shoulders hard beneath her fingertips.

A door swung open and a narrow-faced woman managed a genuine smile.

"Mistress Tessa, I mean, Mistress Hunter." Rachel Briers grabbed hold of both Tessa's hands. "Please, come in. Major Hunter, I have tea hot and ready for you."

"That would be fine. Did you receive the fabric I had sent over from the ship?" How competent and commanding he appeared in an ebony shirt and breeches. A shock of dark hair tumbled over his brow, as black as his gaze that riveted on her. "Tessa has sworn to cooperate."

"I'm perfectly capable of making my own dresses." She blushed, not at all comfortable with such treatment. Goodness, she had been sewing for herself since she was six years of age. But Jonah had explained he wanted to do this for her, because Father's recovery would take time and attention, and she would not have the chance to sew anytime soon.

"Tessa, cooperate?" Rachel hid a smile, though the corners of her mouth upturned with good humor. If there was one person Tessa could call friend in this village, it was Rachel. "I've known her ever since dame school, and not once have I spied a single moment of her cooperative nature. But you, Major Hunter, seem to bring out the best in her."

"Only in public," Tessa piped up, and their laughter rang in the cozy room.

How good it felt here, in Rachel's parlor, safe from the curious gazes of many of the villagers. There was no chance of running into Charity or Violet here either, since Grandfather was not rich enough to hire out the sewing.

"Let me fetch the teapot and we can begin." Rachel spun away, gesturing toward the simple but tidy benches. "Please sit and make yourselves comfortable."

"Let me get the tea." Jonah, so big he shrank the small parlor, gave an awkward but endearing shrug. "You women go ahead and do whatever it is you do."

He tossed her a wink, the devil's own light shining in his eyes. He left her sight, yet the brightness in her heart remained.

"I want you to know I didn't believe one word of those rumors," Rachel whispered, leaning close to grab her sewing box. "I think he truly loves you. Look at these wonderful fabrics he bought you. Sensible cottons, but very finely dyed and woven."

"Aye." Choosing such beautiful cloth while Charity and Violet watched across the table had been a pleasure. 'Twas her pride again, but just this once it felt fine to have more expensive things. "No matter what Jonah says, I want a simple design. Not much different than what I've been wearing."

"He's a man of means, Tessa." Rachel unfolded a length of green linen. "He'll want his wife to dress appropriately."

"Something simple, Rachel. Trust me." Tessa could not imagine wearing a gown too impractical to do her chores in. "I still plan on living as I always have, Jonah's bride or not."

Rachel's lips pursed, but she said nothing more as she lifted the moss green fabric to Tessa's chin. " 'Tis a becoming color on you. I was thinking a bodice and an underskirt of this green, with the floral over it."

" 'Twould be very nice." Tessa tried to imagine how wonderful it would feel to wear such a dress, so different from the drab homespun she'd always worn.

"Tea?" Jonah stood in the threshold, one broad shoulder braced on the doorframe, holding two steaming cups.

His gaze speared hers, so intimate and knowing. She thought of their lovemaking, of her confession, of the silence when he didn't answer.

He had to love her. See how he treated her, all the wondrous cherished words he'd said, standing up for her against Charity, and now buying her such beautiful things when she already had perfectly serviceable dresses.

These were not acts of an unloving man. Unlike her mother, she had not traded security for a cold marriage, a roof over her head in exchange for her usefulness. Jonah could hire nurses or servants. He did not need to marry in order to have someone clear his table or tend his father.

He leaned close, and heat sizzled the back of her neck. "You look beautiful in green."

At his words, the love in her heart doubled once, and then again.

After too much tea and women's talk, Jonah excused himself to the stable, although he was well pleased at Tessa's happiness. She'd not argued overly much at the new clothes, and once she'd stepped foot inside Mistress Briers' parlor, her eyes glimmered with a rare happiness.

Aye, without the mantle of hardship heavy about her slender shoulders, she was a beautiful woman. He wagered others could see it now, too, and he was glad. There were other reasons to have married Tessa, not just for his father's sake. He wanted to protect her, wanted naught but good things for her. After the way she treated him as her husband and how she aided Father, she deserved all he could give her.

Even now, through the open stable door and across the yard, he could see her in the lighted kitchen window. She sat at Rachel's

JONAH'S BRIDE

trestle table, sipping another cup of tea over more talk of ribbons and buttons and bows, no doubt, or whatever it was women discussed.

Even from here, he could see how happiness lit her face, all paleness gone, replaced by rosy cheeks and a quiet smile and eyes that sparkled a vibrant blue. How relaxed she looked, at ease. Her dark hair tumbled out from its braid in places to twist around her heart-shaped face, to brush at her dark collar.

Aye, she deserved all that he could give her. He could not deny a warmth, a feeling that made his chest hurt every time he looked at her.

"Major Hunter." A breathy, childish voice spun him around in the stable. He blinked, the image of Tessa replaced by Violet Bradford. She fluffed styled curls with one hand, plumping them near her face.

A shot of alarm pierced his gut. "Where's your chaperone?"

"My mother, you mean?" Violet tilted her head to one side, working her eyelashes as if a bug had flown into both eyes. "She's currently across the street at Mistress Hollingsworth's."

"Then go there directly."

"But Mama is inquiring about hiring the oldest girl to come work for us. She told me I was in the way." Violet arched her back, seductively, as if to show off her bosom.

"I don't care if she is conferring with the king himself. I want you out of my sight." He dared not be caught alone with a girl like this, and started off on a brisk walk toward the house. He'd seen too much of dark hearts not to recognize one now.

"Everyone knows you were going to propose to me." Violet trotted after him and reached out. "Don't deny it."

He twisted away from her bold touch, anger rising. "I expect you to obey me, little girl. Go find your mother." Violet only smiled. "I know that awful Tessa tricked you into marriage, but that doesn't mean we can't be together."

"Enough!" he roared, hearing his voice echo against the bare-limbed trees.

Violet slapped her hand to her mouth, tears welling in her eyes. "But you c-came by at m-meeting day—"

"To see Tessa, not you."

Tears sluiced down the girl's ruddy face. She turned, wailing, kicking up flecks of earth and mud as she darted across the road and disappeared into the house. A door slammed with a show of temper.

He headed inside the stable, considering Violet Bradford's mistake. Or maybe manipulation. Aye, he was sorely glad he did not give in and choose a woman that young, self-absorbed, and conceited.

The lighted window drew his gaze. He saw Tessa rise from the table, laughter touching her lips. Like ice cracking on a thawing pond, his chest hurt. How it hurt in places long untouched by spring.

* * *

"Tis lucky Mistress Briers had a dress just your size." Jonah's gaze flicked over her, his eyes hot, his smile seductive.

"You should not have bought it." The dress she held in her arms, folded in paper, was too much. But Jonah had insisted. Rachel had sewn the dress for Thankful Bowman, but the Bowmans didn't want the dress after all, now that Major Hunter had chosen a wife.

"Why shouldn't I buy gifts for my wife? I'm glad to do it, Tessa. Besides, you look beautiful in soft colors. Look, we're home. Go upstairs and change into it. I want to see you in something besides homespun."

Her heart beat with love for him. Strong and stoic, his jaw a tight line, he offered her his hand to help her to the ground. His touch was solid, but his eyes were shadowed.

Something troubled him. He treated her well, keeping a hand on her elbow in case she slipped in the mud, although she was perfectly capable of walking by herself, and complimenting her in the wagon when he'd told her how good she'd looked in the colors they had chosen. Yet something was changed.

"Jonah, Tessa." The colonel greeted as they stepped through the door.

Tessa set down her package on the small stand by the door and, still wearing her cloak, marched across the polished floor. "Samuel, I left strict orders for you to stay in bed."

A healthy pink blushed the old man's cheeks.

"Aye, I've not needed to follow orders in a long time. I am sorely out of practice."

"Nay, you're just obstinate, that's what you are." Tessa was not fooled. She loosened the ties on her cloak. "You could catch a chill."

" 'Tis why I am sitting by the fire."

"You are still in danger of overstraining yourself."

" 'Tis why I am sitting in this chair and not dancing around the parlor."

Tessa saw the same devil's gleam in her father-in-law's black eyes. "The lot of you are rogues through and through. What am I to do with you?"

"Are you angry with me, Mistress?" Wide-eyed Anya stepped into the room, a dishtowel twisted between both work-chapped hands. "I told him he was to stay in bed, but he would not listen."

"Nay, I don't blame you. I blame this slick-tongued old man and his sons." So, affection warmed the words. She didn't have the practice in teasing that the men in this family had. "Where are the other guilty parties?"

"Master Thomas is checking on the cows in the stable. Master Andy is upstairs."

Jonah's boots knelled on the wood floor. "Upstairs?"

"Aye, his head is troubling him still." Anya stared hard at the towel she held. "Will you be needing any tea?"

"Nay, Anya." Tessa allowed Jonah to take her cloak, touched at his thoughtfulness. 'Twas good to be loved by such a fine man. "But the colonel will be needing his afternoon medicine."

"Fie on your wicked brews." Samuel waved one big hand, his face crinkling in a show of bitter distaste. "I've not tasted such foulness in my whole life."

"That tea is the reason why you're alive to complain about it." Tessa could not help laughing. "Get accustomed to following my orders, Samuel."

"Why did you have to marry that one? She is fearsome and bossy. Have you not taken the spark out of her yet, boy? Take her to bed some more, then, and wear her out." Humor sparkled in those old eyes.

Tessa blushed and Jonah's hand settled on her shoulder.

"Father, my wife has been too busy tending to a demanding old man who thinks he knows everything. But he doesn't."

The colonel laughed, his chest rumbling, but there was no cough. "It does me good to think I may yet live to see my first grandson. Jonah, fetch me a new book. I've finished this one, and

Andy is resting."

"Tell me which book you prefer." Jonah shouldered over to the bookcase, leaving her side.

She loved the way he walked, strong like a lead wolf, each step one of confidence and power. Her heart ached simply gazing at him. "Anya, are you feeling familiar with the house?"

"Aye." The servant trailed behind her to the kitchen. " 'Tis a larger place than where I came from."

The fragrance of the warm fresh loaves greeted her when she stepped into the kitchen. How tidy everything looked, from the dishes washed and stacked in the glass cupboards to the scrubbed work counter to the clean cloth on the board table. The wood shone from floor to wall to cabinets with the polish of hard work.

"Anya, even I could not have done so much cleaning in just a single day."

"I want you to be happy with me." The pain on the young woman's face reminded Tessa of what it was like to have no home of her own, no family, no one who valued her for more than her work. "This is such a fine position, much better than where I came from."

The contracts for indentured servants could be bought and sold. Tessa had heard mention of how badly some young women were treated. And that was why she chose Anya from the half dozen servants on the ship.

"You must not worry so about earning your place here. And now that you've done more than a day's work and 'Tis hours yet before supper needs to be started, take the rest of the afternoon for yourself."

"But I—"

"Jonah suggested there were old clothes of his sister's stored in the attic. Mayhap you would like to head up there and choose a few more work dresses for yourself, and something nice for church."

"Thank you, mistress." Anya bowed her head and scurried away, her worn homespun skirt snapping with her quick gait.

"Not many fine women married to rich men in this village, or any other for that matter, would treat a servant girl that way." Jonah's lazy step brought him closer.

Her skin heated and prickled, anticipating his touch. "Kindness will not make an industrious person lazy. I've found 'Tis a common misconception."

"Aye." He wrapped his arms around her and drew her full up against his chest. Substantial and hard as steel. She leaned her cheek against his breastbone and heard the dependable beat of his heart. "Father is refusing to drink your tea."

"He can't refuse, Jonah."

"I know. Trust me. I'll find a way to convince him to drink that putrid brew."

"You? I was looking forward to doing battle with the old man." She laughed against him, rejoiced in the vibrating rumbling of his chuckle beneath her ear.

"I hate to deprive you of such fun, but I'm worried about Andy. 'Tis not like him to take to his bed in the middle of the day."

"Mayhap he needs a stronger dose of birch bark tea." She wrapped her arms around her husband and hugged him tight, but when she withdrew, shadows darkened his eyes.

Mayhap he worried about his brother, 'twas only natural. But ever since she had revealed her heart to him, told him she loved him, she feared . . . aye, 'twas only fears. He hadn't answered her then, but hadn't he already confessed his feelings for her when he first proposed? And again many times over in his every word and deed.

"I will see to your brother." She brushed a kiss across his mouth and he kissed her back, fiercely, passionately, erasing any question, any doubts.

Jonah watched his wife disappear in the dark stairwell, her skirts swishing around her slim ankles, then melding with the shadows. Her step brushed light on the wooden stairs above, and he ached at her absence. The new dress he'd bought her from the seamstress sat in its wrapping on the table by the door, forgotten in her haste to see to others.

He could not fault her, for 'twas why he married her. He ought to be glad she lived up to his expectations and made his marriage a good one. But it bothered him too, for Thomas' words and his own shortcomings weighed heavily on his conscience.

Father was recovering and may not be as infirm as the surgeon led them to expect. He looked robust, muttering curses and complaints over Tessa's bird dropping tea. He had seen her grind the herbs himself, but Father tended toward hyperbole.

He was left with a wife who loved him. Who held such tender, magical feelings for him, even after he told her what he was, no hero, no great soldier to esteem, but a man like any other. She still loved him.

"Father, you're not drinking the tea."

"This tastes worse than the mud in the road after haying season when all the horses and oxen have been trodding up and down it." Father's face puckered after another minuscule sip.

" 'Tis one of Tessa's brews that saved your life, you stubborn old man." Thank God for Tessa and her herbs. "You had better do what she says, because I need you alive and well, just as my brothers do."

"Have you tasted this brew?" Sparkles of humor and downright willfulness flicked in the corner of his mouth.

"Nay, although I've heard you describe it in great detail." Wryly, Jonah reached out and caught the cup before Father could upturn it into the hearth.

"Boy, if you value my life, let me accidentally spill this horrid tea."

"I heard that." Tessa swirled into the light, her braid flicking over her shoulder, her dress shivering around her slender woman's curves. Aye, but she looked a sight. "Samuel, spill all the tea you want. I have more."

"She's a feisty one, Jonah. What do you plan to do about it?"

"Hope she never gets mad at me," he teased, but at the lines etched around Tessa's mouth and the way she did not tease back, he tensed. "How's Andy?"

"I'm not certain. He complains of a bad headache, but it doesn't seem to be responding to my herbs."

" 'Tis because your herbs are likely to kill a healthy man," Father spoke up. "Is my son ill?"

"I don't know. He has no fever, no other complaints." Tessa's voice softened. "I know of some roots that when crushed and added with the bark made a powerful pain killer. Andy said he often gets headache, just not this bad."

"I will help you." Jonah rose, leaving his father with a look of warning. "Don't even think about dumping out that tea."

"I could accidentally spill it." The old man looked defiant. "You'll never know."

"A tea that putrid will leave a stain anywhere you pour it."

"And an uncommonly bad smell." Father's humor came thin,

worry wrinkling his face, draining the life from his eyes. "See to Andy. I hope he has not contracted this same illness."

" 'Tis a headache, nothing more." Though Jonah did not feel assured as he went to join Tessa in the kitchen.

She stood at the counter, pestle in hand. A sound variety of earthy smells, of roots and barks and dried leaves, scented the air around her. "Your father thinks I'm torturing him, but he needs to take his medicine for at least one more week. We cannot risk a return of the fever. His lungs are not strong enough to survive another bout of that sickness."

"I know." Jonah laid his hand on her shoulder because he liked touching her. "You have my support. I trust you with my family. With my life."

"Oh, Jonah." She turned and folded herself against his chest and held him so hard. He could feel how much she cared for him. Thomas was right—aye, he'd made a terrible mistake. He had not misled her. He just had never imagined that a practical spinster with more sense than any woman he'd ever met would harbor a heart so tender.

And he would not hurt her. He would never let her know how cold his heart, how desolate. He kissed her brow, those silken curls tickling his chin, and cradled her close. Rain started to tap at the windows, driven by a somber wind.

CHAPTER THIRTEEN

A knock on the front door drew them apart. She hated moving away from him, but she'd given Anya the afternoon off. "I had better answer that before Samuel decides he feels well enough to do it."

"Aye. Let me." He pressed a quick kiss to her brow and then marched away.

Tessa searched through her basket and laid out the crocks on the counter, one by one. She heard the door open and a woman's voice talking fast and high. It sounded like Prudence Bowman.

"Tessa." Jonah pushed through the door, his face tight. "Someone is here to see you. She says her daughter has fallen ill."

A foreboding drew tight in the pit of her stomach. "Send her in—"

"Tessa!" A pale faced woman, dressed in a fine gown and cloak, pushed past Jonah in the threshold and tumbled into the kitchen, windblown and rain specked. "Thankful woke up yesterday saying she didn't feel well, and now she has a fever. She is coughing and fretful."

"What have you been treating her with?" Tessa grabbed up the water pail from the back door and pulled a chair out from the table, motioning Mistress Bowman to sit.

"Honey and tea. My mother swears by it, but it has been of no help." Worry wobbled in her voice as she dropped into the offered chair. "I don't know what else to try."

"I will come take a look as soon as I'm done here." Tessa hefted the heavy pail and poured. Water sluiced into a small kettle. " 'Twill take only a few minutes."

"I fear Thankful's fever is far too advanced. I should have asked for your help earlier, but I was sure it was just from the change in weather and all this dampness."

"Jonah, will you see after Andy?"

While concern narrowed his eyes, he nodded gently. "Thomas has not dragged me out into the fields yet, so I have the time. You want me to give Andy tea?"

"Just plain tea and honey, and he is to drink it all up after he takes this powder. Just this much." She grabbed a spoon from the holder and measured out a quarter teaspoon. "He's to put it right on his tongue. It will taste nasty, but it should ease his pain. If I'm not back by suppertime, make sure he has another cup of tea but no more powder."

"I will." Jonah's hand curled around the kettle handle. "Have Thomas saddle Father's bay mare for you. And Tessa? Try to be home before dark."

A gentle light of caring shone in his eyes, and it moved her, touched her as nothing ever had. He would miss her when she was gone. Her heart filled to brimming. 'Twas a good thing to be loved.

* * *

The sun had set by the time she rode into the stable. The mare was as soaked to the skin as she was. 'Twas a gentle animal, with big friendly eyes and a gentle nature. Friendly, as if the poor animal didn't have anyone to ride her much. Tessa uncinched the saddle and vowed to take the animal out for a run one day soon.

"There you are." Thomas splashed into the stable, wearing a dripping jacket and cap, carrying a small lantern, a tiny beacon against the gathering darkness. "Jonah nearly sent me five different times to see to your safety. He feared the horse had thrown you and left you hurt in the middle of the road."

"I hope you told Jonah I know how to care for myself." Although it warmed her to know her husband worried over her welfare. "Where is he?"

"Putting Father to bed. I saw you ride up." He hooked the lantern on a nail. "Here, let me rub down the mare."

"I was planning on taking her back out again." Tessa gave the horse's neck a gentle pat. "Thankful Bowman complained of a headache yesterday and today she is very ill."

"Andy has a headache." Thomas' jaw tensed. He was a burly man, broader than Jonah through the chest, but not as tall. His somber nature made him seem just as powerful as Jonah, though in a different way. " 'Tis not a good sign."

"Nay. I wanted to take some medicines to Mistress Briers. She complained of a headache today too, and I think 'twould be best to medicate this fever before it hits and settles into the lungs."

"The storm is too miserable. I will take the medicines. All you need to do is write the instructions for the seamstress, and I will see that she gets both."

"You would do that?"

"Aye. Jonah would have my head if I let you back out in that storm. Besides, we fear Andy needs your care now."

Thomas spoke sense, and 'twas good to be needed. And 'twas good to be treated like this, with respect and caring. She imagined this was how good families behaved toward one another, and how nice it was. She knew Thomas, as Jonah's brother, didn't need to come out into the rain to help her or run her errand. But he had.

"Thank you." The words caught in her throat because they were so hard to say.

"For what?" He looked up from grabbing a linen towel from a dark shelf. "For saving you from getting more soaked than you already are?"

"Nay. For accepting me into your family, for treating me so well. 'Tis more than my own family has done." She watched the surprise on his face, and mayhap a bit of confusion. Embarrassed, she ran out into the drumming rain and let the cold wetness sluice away the heat from her face.

"Tessa?" Thomas gazed out at her, framed by the dark threshold, backlit by the single lantern's gentle flame. "I am glad you're happy here with us. We appreciate you more than you know."

Aye, 'twas good to belong. To truly belong. She smiled, not trusting her voice, and hurried to the house. Warmth and the sweet scent of steeping tea met her as she rushed inside. Water dripped from her cloak's hem.

"Mistress." Anya spun from the hearth. "We've all been

worried. The storm is so severe."

"No need to worry, for I'm well. Has Andy shown any signs of fever?"

"Nay, but he has been coughing." The girl stuffed her hands behind a pretty but plain apron. "Colonel Hunter said that since I was looking around in the attic as you told me to do, I should take whatever I might need. Like this apron."

Tessa knew Anya had come with only the clothes on her back. "Did Samuel climb the attic ladder by himself?"

"Aye. He tried to swear me to secrecy, but I told him I would not lie to my mistress." A small nervous smile flickered across her pale face. "If this is too much, I can put it back."

"Nay, an apron is sensible. And we must clothe you. Think of how indecent it would be if we did not." On a smile, Tessa shrugged out of her cloak and hung it on a wall peg to drip dry. "Do you like your room?"

" 'Tis very comfortable. With a real bed. The colonel said I might borrow a book to read at night from the library after my work was done. If I am careful with it. Is that all right?"

"Of course. I would let you go now, but I need help with an onion poultice for Andy."

"Let me go down cellar and fetch some onions. How many will you need?"

"Four will do." Tessa reached up into the cupboard and found a small empty crock. The girl had already slipped into the pantry. The cellar door squealed a protest in the small room.

Tessa measured out a good amount of crushed yarrow leaves, sweetgrass, dried bearberries, cottonwood bark, and mint. She set Anya to peeling, then slicing the onions. Thomas knocked at the back door, and she handed him a small packet with instructions, wrapped in leather to protect it from the rain. She thanked him again, and he was gone, blending into the shadows of the thunderous night.

She chose cottonwood bark to steep with Andy's tea and then headed upstairs. The house seemed quiet with the parlor dark and the colonel asleep.

At the head of the stairs, a thin light drew her to Andy's chamber. The door was ajar. She could see a bed centering the room where a down comforter was drawn up to Andy's chin. A fire crackled in the small fireplace, the light glancing over Jonah to illuminate the sleeping man propped up by pillows.

"How is Mistress Thankful?"

"Not well. Her malady seems similar to your father's. Is Andy worse?"

"Aye, he started coughing after supper. Not hard, and he doesn't have the rattle in his chest Father had." Lines furrowed across Jonah's brow. How tired he looked, how worried. He'd pulled his dark hair back into a leather tie at his nape. If he were not in a sick room, he could be mistaken for a pirate, or mayhap a spy for the French. His hand caught hers and fire skidded across her skin. Desire built in her blood. "I didn't send for you because I knew Mistress Thankful was more ill."

"Anya is slicing onions for a poultice. It will help keep his lungs clear." Tessa watched Jonah rise and tower his full height over her. She stepped into the shelter of his arms, against the wondrous comfort of his chest. She could hold him forever just like this with their hearts beating together.

"Andy will be ecstatic. He sleeps now, but when he was awake he complained mightily of your awful tasting headache powder." His hand on her back caressed slow circles at her spine. "I scared him into taking it by saying I would fetch you from the Bowmans."

She tilted her face upward, and his smile became a kiss, fiery and possessive.

"I missed you this evening." His fingers brushed over her hips. How dark his eyes were. Was he thinking of the last time they'd made love? How she straddled him, brushed by only candlelight and his hands, and took his hard shaft inside her?

"Tell me how ill Andy is." How rough his voice sounded, low and intimate. Aye, he was thinking of it, too. "Then we'll see what comes next between us."

He stepped away, and the ache for him low in her belly grew heavier. She craved him, like air and water and sleep. She wanted to make love to this man who'd given her not just a home and a place to belong, but his love. 'Twas all she had wished for, prayed for, dreamed of.

Tessa drew the chair up to the bed and set the burning taper on the nearby stand. Light washed Andy's face, slack and younger looking in sleep. A slight blush pinkened his cheeks. The color was high, near his eyes, and a faint trace of it painted his brow.

"He doesn't feel overly warm, but the fever has begun."

So, there would be no pleasure this night. She would do all she could to help Andy fight the fever, which like Thankful Bowman, struck more swiftly than with the colonel. 'Twas why she feared it would be all the more dangerous. "I'll need another candle, Jonah. And wood for the fire."

A muscle jumped in his jaw. His beautiful shoulders tensed. "As you wish, my lady." He kissed her brow, tenderly this time, so infinitely tender.

'Twas going to be a long night.

He heard the outside door close down below, for the kitchen was beneath Andy's room. The fire burned low, in need of more wood, its orange-red glow lashing the fine cut of Tessa's back and the slender shape of her shoulders. The back of her neck, bent over her work, looked vulnerable. Dark curls that had escaped her braid gathered there, ebony silk against creamy satin.

"What do you need from the kitchen?"

"I could use more clean dish towels."

"I'll be right back." He pressed a kiss to her forehead. A warm feeling beat in his chest as he stepped away. She returned to her work, checking the poultice smeared on Andy's chest.

The hallway was cool, the parlor damp and cold. Spring came stubbornly this year, holding back its warmth. "Thomas, is that you?"

"Aye. I've brought in more wood."

Jonah studied his brother, face lined and brow furrowed, and recognized that dark brooding look. "I thought you had gone to bed."

"Andy is my brother, too." Thomas knelt before the wood box, instead of nosily dumping his armload, and quietly filled the copper tub stick by stick.

"You looked troubled. Is it Andy? The fever is a serious one." Jonah bent to help.

"Aye, Andy's illness does worry me, but something else also troubles me." He set the last chunk of maple into the box, then dusted the slivers of wood, bark, and moss from his gloves and jacket. "Do you know what Tessa did today?"

"She did many things." Jonah turned to sort through the shelves beneath the work counter.

"She thanked me."

"Thanked you?" He spied the towels and grabbed a couple. "Pray, tell me 'Tisn't so! It must have tortured you. What did you do to deserve such treatment?"

"Offered to take medicine to Mistress Briers for her, because of the storm." Thomas walked to the window just as lightning split the sky, flashing behind the curtain. Thunder rolled overhead, angry and ear splitting. "But that wasn't all she thanked me for. She's grateful for how well we treat her. For how I treat her."

"So, you feel guilty, is that it? Do you feel bad for wagering Andy five pounds over my choice in a wife?"

"Do not tease, brother. I'm not proud of myself. I only meant to jest. Why, Tessa is an honest woman, but there isn't one man in all of Connecticut Colony who could see the Tessa Bradford you married. I have come to like her, and I respect her for what she does."

"As do I."

"She brought our father back to us, when the surgeon had no hope. And now Andy is ill, and she is up there right now at his side, no matter that 'Tis midnight and she's had little sleep to call her own."

"You're telling me what I already know."

Lightning flashed, thunder rattled the windowpanes. Thomas hefted the curtain away from the glass and stared out at the black sheets of rain. "She thinks we treat her well, and my conscience bothers me. How it bothers me. But what troubles me more is that my brother, the great heroic Major Hunter, reported to save innocent colonists from marauding Indians, is using this goodhearted woman."

"I am *not* using her." Defensive rage flared in his chest, more striking than the lightning searing the night.

"Then what do you call it? You should have hired a nurse, Jonah. Not married that poor woman. She thinks you love her," Thomas scolded over the raging thunder.

"I do happen to care about her." Jonah tossed down the towels to clench his hands. "She's my wife, and none of your concern."

"What goes on in front of my nose is my concern." Thomas spun from the window, and a single bayberry candle illuminated the fight in his eyes. "She has done naught but care for every member in this family since she arrived here. Aye, and she even cares for a penniless servant. She believes you love her, Jonah, and new dresses and decent treatment do not excuse how you lie to her and deceive her. She thinks she has your heart."

"Aye, but how can I say such a thing to her?" Troubled, Jonah faced the window, studying the night-black windowpanes and his own reflection within. "It would hurt her terribly, and that is why she can't know. I may have chosen to marry her because she could take care of Father, but that's not why I want her to stay. I—"

Something clattered to the floor behind him. A silence settled on the room. Not even the thunder above dared to intrude. Jonah felt her presence like a touch to his back, like a mark on his conscience.

"Look how clumsy I am." She knelt to the floor, retrieving the fallen bowl. She turned away so that the nighttime shadows cloaked her face. Her hands worked quickly. "Jonah, you took so long for the towels. 'Tis time to take the paste off Andy's chest."

Her hands shook as she set the bowl on the counter.

Damn his stupid tongue. "Tessa." He stepped forward.

She sidestepped. "I need only a bit of wash water." She poured water from the lukewarm kettle into her shallow bowl. Her voice sounded thick with unshed tears. "Whilst there is still no fever, 'Tis best to be cautious."

"Tessa, you misunderstand. I did not mean those words the way they sounded." He had only wanted to keep her from hurting, to protect her caring heart.

Tessa was a person, his wife, with feelings deep and true, and he had been wrong to think an unwanted spinster who worked for a roof over her head would be merely glad to live in a big house and have a life of ease. She had dreams and needs and a heart large enough to spend her days and nights caring for those in the village who were ill or dying. Many accepted her help only to tease her or judge her when it suited, and all without payment, without reward.

She was a woman who had offered to care for his dying father out of gratitude, out of a kindness Father had shown to her mother many years ago.

Those were not sensible actions, but deeds of a deeply feeling heart.

"Tessa, let me explain." He could make this right, he knew he could. He was not using her. Not for his pleasures in bed, not as a nurse for his family. Tessa was his wife and he was both proud and pleased with her. He would give her more—his whole heart—if he had it to give.

But she scooped up the towels and the basin and hurried off, her gait efficient and sensible.

"I don't think she will forgive you," Thomas predicted.

As if in agreement, lightning split the shadowed light between them and thunder shattered the night.

Her hands trembled as she cleaned the dried mash of onions and herbs from Andy's chest. He woke with a murmur, then went back to sleep. Not yet sick, but a fever on the way. She dried his chest and covered him well. She could do no more for now.

She felt numb clear to the bone as she folded the soiled towels and set them by the door for Anya to gather in the morning. And that numbness grew as she blew out the candle and crept through the room. A glow from the dying fire tossed light at her feet and she stepped out into the unlit corridor, her mood just as dark.

She heard footsteps on the staircase, tapping slowly. Jonah's gait, Jonah's step. Her pulse drummed in her ears, fast and hollow. She listened to the knell of his boots against the floor silence outside Andy's chamber, then progress down the corridor.

"Tessa?"

She turned toward the chest of drawers. A spear of lightning flashed, and a second of white light illuminated the wooden handle of the hairbrush. Darkness returned and her fingers curled around the worn handle.

"May I ask what you heard?"

"Enough." She flicked her braid over shoulder and tugged at the ribbon. The bow loosened.

"I'm sorry for what I said. I'm glad you are my wife, regardless of what you heard."

"I bet you are." She dropped the small bit of ribbon on the chest of drawers and ran her fingers through the plaiting to loosen it. "Your father is well. 'Tis what you wanted. What you bartered your future for."

"That's not true and you know it." His voice twisted, rang low and solemn. His footsteps drummed on the floor, then whispered on the braid carpet "I am well pleased with you. Surely you know that."

"I don't know what to believe." She shook her hair out.

"You can believe that I care about you." His hands curled around her shoulders, possessive, as if he were afraid to let go of her.

"Fine. You care about me. You care that I tend your father." She shrugged away from his touch and faced him, the numbness in her heart remaining, but anger was starting to smolder. "I would have stood by him anyway, without being married to you. But I suppose you couldn't understand that, not the great Jonah Hunter, not a man who can buy anything he wishes. Who thinks he can *buy* affection."

"There's only a certain type of affection for sale, and that is the kind I wanted to avoid." His jaw was set, but his eyes, how tenderness lived there and regret as black as midnight.

"What of Violet Bradford?" he demanded. "Do you think I'd rather have one such as her? She caught up to me in Mistress Briers' stable to make an indecent offer. Nay, I don't want a shallow woman, no matter how young and beautiful, to look at me and see only their betterment."

" 'Tis what you gave me in exchange for other services." Let him try to be rational, to explain, to regret she had learned the truth. She walked around him, fisting her hands, trembling and torn between wanting to rail at him and wanting to leave. "You took me into your bed, Jonah. When all you wanted was a nurse."

"Nay, I won't let you do this. I made love with you in this bed and I'll not erase what happiness we've found here. I gave you what heart I have, and 'Tis far more than I have given any woman."

"New clothes, a servant, a fine house to live in—"

"Nay." Rich as midnight that voice, as inviting as dreams. He stood behind her but did not touch her, though his presence burned like an ember, smoldering first, then licking hotter.

Still, her heart remained numb, as if a physical injury had left her unable to feel. Shock, 'twas all. And then, in time would come the pain. "Do you deny it?"

"Deny what? Wanting you the way a man wants a woman? You know I did before I proposed to you."

"You thought I had a lover and was experienced to your advances. Your indecent advances." The quaking low in her midsection spread and grew.

"I wanted you then, Tessa, and I want you now. Naught has changed. Father was a hair's breadth from dying, and you know how close. So I decided on a standard, that is all. And 'twas stupid, I agree. But it led me to you."

"A standard? I thought you married me because—" She paused. "Because you loved me."

"Aye. And I am learning. Give me time, Tessa. I'm only beginning to learn."

Apology rang low and sincere in his voice. He thought he'd done little wrong. And mayhap, to another, what he'd done could be easily forgiven. But he had fed her dreams, made her believe...

She squeezed her eyes shut. "You chose to marry me because you also thought I could not love. Is that right?"

"Aye. I don't want to lie to you. 'Tis one of my greatest flaws and I never wanted you to know."

"I see." A tuft of pain scratched inside her chest and she fought it, tamped it down, turned off her heart.

She would not let him know how foolish she'd been, just how much he'd duped her. Nay, she'd duped herself.

Believing a man as handsome and wondrous and envied by all could love her, a horse-faced, sharp-tongued spinster, according to many who had no problem telling her the truth.

"Tessa?" Thomas' knock on the door drew her around. "The reverend is in the parlor. Seems a little girl at the Hollingsworth household is burning with fever. He has come to request your help."

"Of course I'll come." Her decision was clear. She could not look at Jonah as she snatched the ribbon for her hair. "Let me grab my basket. Thomas, please tell the reverend to meet me outside."

"Tessa, we must finish this. I don't want you to leave like this."

"A little girl needs me. Truly needs me. Unlike you." She could not bear to look at her husband, at the man she had foolishly thought could love her. She turned and walked away.

The storm faded, and with every passing hour the silence felt more ominous. Jonah sat in the parlor, the dark broken only by a beam of moonshine through the part in the curtains.

"Conscience troubling you?" Thomas shouldered into the room.

"I thought you were upstairs."

"Nay, I could not sleep. I checked on Andy, then I went to the stable to think." A loose floorboard creaked as Thomas ambled closer. "You hurt her, Jonah."

"Aye. She wasn't meant to hear those words. I should not have spoken so freely." He steepled his hands, resting his elbows on his knees. "In time, she'll understand."

"A woman doesn't understand something like that. They are emotional creatures."

"Tessa is sensible. She will forgive me."

"Jonah, many in this village are bitter. Many a father had hoped it would be his daughter living in this house married to the rich and heroic major. Many feel Tessa unfairly took their chance away. You know what they have been saying. She has, too, and probably believes it now."

"I know." And he despised anyone who spoke against his wife, his good-hearted wife. Before her, he had forgotten what happiness felt like, that there was goodness in the human heart.

"She will be exhausted when she returns." Thomas pulled back the edge of the curtain and peered outside. "I would think on that, if I were you."

" 'Tis my plan." As long as he lived, he would make this up to Tessa, prove to her he wanted her and no other for his wife.

But as the hours ticked by, it began to feel as if she wasn't returning, as if she would never come home again.

CHAPTER FOURTEEN

Six-year-old Mercy Hollingsworth worsened as the night faded to dawn. Her fever raged, dampening the gold ringlets at her brow, and everything Tessa tried merely slowed the fever, did not stop it. Mercy's lungs filled until she couldn't draw more than the faintest of breaths.

The reverend prayed beside the father and mother at the foot of the bed while Tessa worked. She crushed herbs and made poultices and compresses intended to bring down the fever and loosen the congestion in the lungs. Nothing worked. Not one thing.

"I cannot lose her," Susan sobbed.

She and Susan had gone to school together and had been in the same class. They had grown apart when Tessa's mother grew ill and she no longer attended school or socials or parties or regular meetings. Mother had needed her, but Susan had always remained kind, unlike many others.

Glancing around the small parlor where the child's bed had been brought down close to the fire, she saw the touches of a loving family—finger painted masterpieces by the little girls tacked on the walls, a doll on a bench in the corner and beneath it toys huddled in a small pile. Such a priceless life Susan had.

Pain wedged into an unyielding ball in her throat and Tessa blinked away unwanted tears. Mercy coughed, and Tessa held her gently. Susan crept close and she handed the child to her mother, the poor thing so fevered she did not know who held her.

"I can see it in your eyes, Tessa." Susan's face crumpled. "I'm going to lose her."

"I can't lie to you." Tessa's throat ached with sadness. "I can think of only one thing to try, a stronger dose of blackbale root. 'Tis a dangerous level, but at this point she'll not recover anyway."

"You know we can't afford a surgeon, but if that would save Mercy—"

"Nay, he wouldn't get here in time. Besides, I have never noticed much improvement from bleeding. If it comes to that, I can do it myself." She hurt for Susan, for this precious child she stood to lose. "She needs more cool compresses. Like this."

She showed Susan how to apply them, then hurried to the kitchen to crush more roots into powder. As she worked, a tiny girl crawled down the ladder in her flannel nightdress, her cap askew revealing bountiful gold curls.

"Whatcha doin'?" the child asked as both stockinged feet hit the floor.

"Making medicine for your sister." Tessa knelt down, her roots forgotten, to admire the child, still plump with baby fat, her eyes as blue as berries. "Is your other sister up in the attic sleeping, too?"

A serious nod. "Julia's a slug 'cuz she won't get outta bed."

"I see." Tessa spied a crock and peered inside it. Just as she suspected. Cookies. She snatched two and held them out for the little girl. "Why don't you go sit at the table and eat these? I need to talk to your mama."

"Thank you." Delight shone in those eyes, for what a treat cookies were before breakfast.

But 'twas the only thing Tessa could think of to keep the child from the sick room. "Susan?"

The woman sat on the bed, leaning over her dying daughter, applying the cold cloths to her fever-raged body. She looked up and, as if she could tell from the tone in Tessa's voice, tears welled. "No, not my other girls."

"Julia is upstairs. I need to go check on her. I want your husband to take little Judith over to your mother's house and keep her there in isolation. She doesn't yet look flushed. Mayhap she will not fall ill."

"Zeb!" She flew at her husband, panic sharp in her voice, for she knew this illness could take all her children.

Tessa checked on Judith, who was just starting in on her second cookie, and then quietly climbed the ladder. She spied a small lump in the bed. "Julia, I hear you are feeling poorly."

"Aye, is that you, Mistress Tessa?"

" 'Tis. Remember when I tended your fever last winter?"

"I do. You made me better."

"Aye. Let me feel your forehead now."

The child's brow was indeed warm.

Tessa smoothed Julia's unruly curls, sadness filling her. A deadly illness was sweeping through the village. Her problems felt small in comparison.

Dawn teased at the curtains in Andy's room, a gray dreary light that promised a rain-filled day. Jonah dusted the slivers of bark from his shirt and straightened away from the hearth as the flames greedily licked at the new wood.

"Where is Tessa?" Andy asked from his bed. "I'm surprised she is not here to torture me with more of that evil brown powder."

"She was called to the Hollingsworth home late last night and we have not heard from her since. One of the girls is ill." Jonah tugged the chair sideways and sat on it. "You look fevered. Your face is flushed."

"I sure don't feel like getting out of bed." Andy stared at the ceiling, looking troubled. "But I have no time to be sick. I have to help you thick-skulled oafs turn the sod in the fields to get it ready for planting."

"Aye, Thomas and I are dolts and we would not know where to start without you to show us." Jonah scooped a dipper of water from the small pail and poured it into an empty cup on the nightstand. "Drink this. I'll have Anya bring your breakfast to you."

And he would fetch Tessa home. Andy worsened. And besides, they had much to discuss. He didn't like how they parted last night with her running off in a cold temper, even if it was to help a sick child.

"Thomas, mayhap we should head to the Hollingsworths' house and see if they are in need of anything."

"I know what you're up to. You just want to try to make things right with your wife." Thomas clomped into the room with a cup of steaming tea. "From Anya. Tessa left it behind for you, Andy, and it smells powerfully bad."

"Oh, joy." Andy made a face, then stopped to cough. "I had hoped without her here, I could escape her bird dropping tea."

"And she scared Anya into the importance of your drinking it, so I suspect she will be up here shortly with some ruse to check and make sure you didn't dump it into the chamber pot." Thomas handed the cup to his littlest brother.

Jonah laughed. "I hear footsteps on the stairs."

" 'Tis her, Andy. Drink it quick, else she will tell Tessa." Thomas teased.

Andy doubled over with a fit of coughing, nearly spilling the tea. Jonah swiped the cup from his hands and held it far away so he did not need to breathe in the horrid aroma from the steam.

Anya rushed into the room carrying a tray of corn pone and poached eggs and fragrant sausages. Her pale face flushed as they watched her unload the plates and bowls, and he realized she had brought food for all of them.

"And I served your father as well," she said quietly, chin bowed to avoid eye contact. She looked more rested today without the bruised fatigue beneath her eyes. She had looked like little more than a skeletal waif on the ship's deck in a worn dress that looked as if it could be patched no more.

Now, she wore a simple muslin dress that had been their sister's long ago, a light yellow fabric with sprinkles of tiny budded roses. 'Twas too large for her narrow frame, and birdlike, she practically hopped to the door. "I know 'Tis wrong of me to presume, but mayhap I could take a meal basket to Mistress Tessa. She has worked the night through and that means the child is so ill she cannot leave her side. I know, for my mother was a healer once, too."

Jonah had wondered if the Hollingsworth child was gravely ill. 'Twas the only reason he hadn't charged over there to speak with Tessa and soothe her temper. " 'Tis a good idea, Anya. Prepare the basket and we'll take it over to her."

"Might I add more for the family? In times such as this, no one has the heart to cook, yet they must eat to keep up their strength."

"Aye, that would be fine."

He watched Andy's face change as the servant left the room. His cough had stopped, but his face was red and strained with pain. "Thomas, did Tessa leave any more medicine?"

"Nay. She wanted to see how he was before she administered more."

Jonah handed the tea to Andy. "I know. It smells like a wet rat, but there is naught to be done but to drink it. It should give you enough piss and vinegar to chase pretty Anya around the kitchen."

"If I did, Tessa said she'd have my head, and I believe her. Your wife may be a kitten when it comes to you, but she is still fearsome when riled." Andy took a sip of his tea and choked. "You cannot imagine how powerfully putrid this tastes."

"Drink it." Thomas crossed his arms over his chest and braced his feet against the floor. "I'll not have my brother become more ill."

Jonah caught Thomas' gaze and read the concern there. Aye, he had worries, too.

"I'll saddle the horses." Jonah stood. Keeping his hands busy would make him less likely to worry over the dangerous work Tessa did, tending to those who were ill, and how he wished he had last night to do over again.

The pain in his heart reminded him she was gone. He couldn't believe it hurt so much to be without Tessa in his life.

"She feels a bit cooler." Tessa laid her cheek against Mercy's forehead just to make sure. "Aye, she does. Susan, the fever is retreating."

"Praise Heaven." Susan crumpled to her knees at the bedside, unshed tears finally falling. "Oh, Zeb. Did you hear? Mercy is going to live."

"Aye, and all because of Mistress Hunter's care." Grief eased from his rough face as he knelt down beside his wife, taking her in his sturdy arms.

Tessa dropped her gaze to give the couple privacy as she dunked another cloth in the herbed water and wrung excess moisture from it. There was still the lung fluid to be dealt with, but the onion poultice had helped the colonel. Tessa thought it would do the same for little Mercy.

A knock rattled the door. Zeb stood. "I wager that is the reverend. He's back from his duties at the meetinghouse."

A cool wind slung through the cabin, making the fire flicker when he opened the door. "Major Hunter. Have you come looking for your wife?"

"Aye. And our Anya has made breakfast for all of you, thinking you wouldn't have time with a sick child to care for." Jonah's voice rumbled with warmth, with a spine-tingling richness. Tessa folded the cloth in thirds, deliberately keeping her back to the door, both to block the child from the wind and to stop herself from turning around to face him. To keep from letting him see her heart in her eyes, her foolish, dreamer's heart.

"How thoughtful." Susan swiped the tears from her eyes. "With two ill children, I haven't given a thought to cooking. Come in, Major Hunter."

She heard his boots knell on the floor and the click of the latch catching as the door closed. The room felt warmer with him in it. She gazed down at the sleeping child. Another touch to her brow proved the fever was truly fading.

Encouraged, Tessa concentrated on her work and kept her back to her husband. She did not want to be distracted from doing her best for little Mercy, not even if her own heart was breaking. She heard the low voices of Anya and Susan talking in the kitchen and the rumble of the men in conversation right behind her, and the pop from the blazing fire in the hearth. Still, Jonah's low voice drew her thoughts away from her work.

Although she felt ready to crack in two, her body heated, knowing he stood an arm's length away. All she would have to do was reach out and he would take her against his strong chest and hold her until the fear and the pain subsided. But she could not allow it. She would not be a fool twice.

She knelt to uncover the frying pan on the floor at her feet and scooped a goodly amount of onion mash into a spoon. She gently set the heated paste on Mercy's chest.

"I often helped my mother." Anya knelt on the other side of the bed, across from Tessa, the little girl between them. "She knew much about tending the sick. 'Tis necessary to have at least one healing woman in a village."

"I could use help. I've two girls here to tend, and Thankful Bowman to check on. How's Andy?"

"Worsening, but I think the tea is helping him fight it. He doesn't seem as ill as this one."

"Aye, but he may. I will send another mixture home with Jonah. If you wouldn't mind spreading this poultice, then I can see how little Julia fares."

"I have applied these before." Anya no longer looked shy but competent, sure of her skills. She had tender hands, slim and careful. She would do a good job, Tessa knew.

Avoiding Jonah, she climbed upstairs to see Julia. She did not wish to move the child yet, who slept cozy beneath several quilts, her fever not yet dangerously high. She would crush more roots and maybe make a strong poultice. It worked for Mercy's aggressive fever. Mayhap Tessa could stop the illness before it made Julia as sick.

When she climbed down the ladder, Jonah was there. Oh, apology was plain on his face. He thought he could smile at her, that she would be grateful enough for a good home and a husband better than Horace Walling, and that would be all. He couldn't see how his motives mattered.

He would soon see how wrong he was.

"Have some breakfast. You need to keep up your strength." He held out a cup of tea, steaming and fragrant. "You look far too pale."

"From lack of sleep and from you." She said it low, without accusation. For in truth, half of the blame was hers. She was at fault for believing his lies, for imagining this man could love a woman like her.

He winced. "I had hoped for some quick forgiveness."

"Go on and hope. I'll not stop you." She plucked the tea from his grip and sipped it, retreating to her work space on Susan's polished counter.

Jonah's hands settled on her shoulders. "I'm proud of you, Tessa. This work you do, 'Tis courageous. It takes a strength of character to sit beside the dying and not run, not be afraid."

"I am often afraid," she confessed, unclasping the lid from a crock. "But such is life, Jonah. 'Tis scary business. The birthing and the dying and all that comes in between. 'Tis not only in legends of war heroes, but in the strength of quietly living and loving and trusting."

Jonah saw it then, how completely he'd failed her. There was nothing wrong with setting a criterion for a wife, using it to choose his bride. The wrong came in letting her believe she was special to him, that she was above price, beyond his own fear to trust and love another. Those gifts, that courage, he hadn't given her.

Because he was afraid to hand over his heart to another, to feel emotions that could make him vulnerable, like he was at this moment.

'Twas all she could do to gather enough courage to walk through the door. She lingered on the road outside the impressive clapboard house with a dozen black-paned windows glimmering in the weak sun.

Overnight it seemed as if the earth had been reborn. Tiny gray buds dotted black-limbed trees, promises of the leaves yet to come. And on the ground, when she looked closely, tiny shoots of green struggled beneath the dirt and last year's grasses. Birds sang more loudly, as if rejoicing in the change of season. Even the afternoon air smelled different, filled with promise.

Tessa narrowed her gaze to the house. She could see the colonel's room, the curtains open to take advantage of the view of forestland and the river beyond. A great fondness for the old man penetrated the cold shock still clamped around her heart She knew Samuel would be hurt, but it could not be helped.

Gathering what strength she could, she pushed open the door and stepped inside the house that would no longer be her home. The parlor was empty, although a fire crackled in the hearth. A book lay closed on the chair between the fireplace and the window where the colonel liked to read. He was probably upstairs taking a needed nap.

She did not bother to take off her cloak, for she would be leaving soon. More numbness crept over her, and she felt as she had when her mother finally died, unable to feel anything at all. But this numbness wouldn't last long, she knew that, too, as ice on a pond could never stay frozen. In time, spring always came.

Andy slept in his bed, a hot fire snapping in the grate. She set her basket down quietly and laid a hand to his brow. Aye, there was a fever, but it wasn't as intense as the colonel's had been, or little Mercy Hollingsworth's.

Encouraged, she snatched her basket of herbs and headed down the hall where the door stood open. She paused in the threshold to see the bed carefully made, Anya's work, and the curtain thrown back to let the meager sun gleam through the window.

It took no time at all to pack, for she'd hardly had the chance to unpack. Her mother's wedding gown, the dress she had worn to become Jonah's wife, was already folded in paper on top of the few keepsakes she owned, Mother's hymnal, her book of prayers, a treasured volume of Shakespeare's sonnets.

Tessa gently brushed this last book with the tips of her fingers. 'Twas the only remembrance she had of her father, of the man whose love Mother had talked about and treasured all of her life. Tessa had wanted to find a man like that, but poetry and dreams did not make love. Only two caring hearts could.

She gathered her hairbrush and pins, the cap and nightdress and underthings from the chest of drawers. A dull ache settled between her brows and behind her eyes. She rubbed the tense muscles there and then clasped the trunk lid tight.

There, she was packed, ready to go. 'Twas a little trunk and didn't weigh more than a sack of grain. She hefted it in both hands and carried it down the corridor, passing the colonel's room.

She heard a clatter in the kitchen and set the trunk down out of the way of the door. What if that was Jonah? How could she face him?

He'd been so confident this could be fixed between them, judging by the way he treated her at the Hollingsworths'. Fixing her a breakfast plate, bringing her tea, and when he left, promising to check on her before nightfall. He worked hard to convince her he cared, that much was true.

But simple caring was not enough. Not now. Not with the way her heart ached for his touch, for all of him.

He'd made her love him with his acts of caring. Now such a bright affection burned in her heart, her days would be dark without it.

How did she deny her feelings? She could not embrace Jonah Hunter's idea of a practical marriage.

But 'twas Thomas in the kitchen, heating tea for Andy. From the dark warmth in his eyes and the set of his chin, he must know all that had happened. Aye, he'd probably known from the start, being Jonah's confidant.

What did he think of her? Did he look at her and see a woman desperate enough to imagine love where there was only resignation? To call home a place where she was only needed for her useful skills?

Recalling how she'd thanked him in the stable that day for coming to care for her mount and to run her errand, she blushed and could not meet his gaze.

"Here is more powder for Andy. Anya will be home soon to administer it. I have already told her how much to give him. And these are the herbs for the compresses. And this for the tea. Do not mix them. One is to help strengthen the blood, and the other to fight the congestion in his lungs."

Thomas took the offered packets, already carefully measured. "You will not stay and tend him yourself? Or does the Hollingsworth girl need you more?"

"I'll come and check on him, as I would anyone else." She took a step toward the door, staring hard at the floorboards. "My trunk is in the parlor. Will you see that it is delivered to my grandfather's home?"

"Are you leaving us?" How low his voice, and his kindness hurt-Aye, how it hurt. "This is not my home, not truly. Violet and my step grandmother have fallen ill, so I am welcome there for now."

"Then allow me to see you home." His hand settled on the doorknob before she could turn it. "If you ever have need of anything, and I mean it, then you come to me. Not because you saved my father's life, but because I will always consider you my sister."

Those were kind words, and she knew Thomas meant them. Somehow, she found the breath in her too-tight chest to speak. "The hardest thing about leaving is knowing I'll no longer have brothers to tease."

He laughed then, making her leaving easier. She stepped out into the sunlight and smelled spring in the air.

After leading the oxen in from the fields, he headed toward the house. Judging by the sun slung low over the treetops it was nearly suppertime. He wanted to drive Anya over to the Hollingsworths' to bring Tessa her meal.

The back door banged open to reveal an empty kitchen. Leather pouches sat on the counter near the hearth. He recognized them. Tessa used them to store some of her roots and things in. Had she been here?

Thomas was nowhere to be found. Father was in the parlor, reading.

"Heard that wife of yours is saving lives left and right again."

Natural color was back in the man's face, and the snap of fight back in his manner. "I saw her leave with Thomas. I gave Andy the bird dropping tea, just like I promised. I made him drink every drop."

"How is he?"

"Feverish, but Tessa looked in on him. Thomas said she thought he had a light case, nothing to fear as long as we take good care of him." Father's nose turned toward his book. " 'Tis good to have a healer in the family. Will come in handy when your babe is sick, as babes are wont to be."

"Aye." Father didn't seem to know of the problems between him and Tessa, and he was grateful. He headed toward the stairs, but that troubled feeling wrapped tight around his guts worsened.

He'd been out in the field since dinner and had been visible from the house. If she had been here, why hadn't she come out to see him? Why hadn't Thomas come to fetch him and let him know she was here, able to finally talk?

The chamber felt strangely empty. It felt as if all the light had gone from the room. He couldn't explain the feeling. Troubled, he pulled off his muddy shirt and shucked off his breeches. Something definitely didn't feel right

He tugged open a drawer and saw the empty place where Tessa's brush and comb had been. He turned and saw the old trunk gone from the place against the wall. An icy chill shivered down his spine.

Pain as cold as an iceberg rammed through his chest. Jonah staggered. It couldn't be. Tessa could not have left. This was her home. She was his wife. There had to be some other explanation.

But none other came to him. Not a single one.

A horrible renting emptiness tore him apart, worse than any Indian's sharpened arrowhead. It surely could not be his heart hurting, for he had no heart. No heart vulnerable to love, that is.

He grabbed clean clothes from the drawers, dressing as he charged down the hall.

"Tessa!" A furious pounding rattled Grandfather's back door, nearly shaking it off the leather hinges. "Tessa, open up, damn it!"

"Jonah!" She pulled the latch and swung open the door just before his upraised fist slammed into it again. "Stop cursing and lower your voice. There are sick people in this house."

"Where is your trunk?" He pushed past her, tense male might and sizzling rage.

Tessa took one look at the power bunched in his arms, tensed in his shoulders, and her heart stopped. "In my attic room. Where it belongs."

"Belongs? Nay, your place is with me. I mean it. To run out like this, 'Tisn't right. We haven't even tried to speak of this."

"What do we have to discuss? You wanted a nursemaid for your father and you found one. He's recovering now. What need do you have of me?"

A light flickered in his eyes, a dark and dangerous light. "I thought you were very clear on the different ways I need you."

"Aye, you need a woman. There are more than a dozen in this town hungering for a man like you. 'Tis best that you leave, Jonah. I no longer want to be your convenient wife."

"You are the least convenient person I know."

"Good, then you're finally rid of your difficult wife." She splayed both hands on his chest and shoved hard. "You should be glad."

"I'm not glad." He didn't budge.

She shoved again, but he was an unmovable pillar of steely muscle and furious determination. How did she think she could move him? "I never want to see you again, so get out of this house."

"Never." His fingers curled around her wrists, holding her hard, just short of bruising. "Not without you."

"What are you going to do? Use force? Haul me over your shoulder?"

A spark lit his eyes as if she'd given him an idea. "All I want is for you to listen to me. I can make you understand—"

"Make me? What would you have me do? Live the rest of my life looking over the breakfast table at a man who will never love me in return? Spend the rest of my nights making love to a man who is only taking his pleasure with me? Spend my days being useful instead of feeling loved in return?"

"Tessa, I truly care for you." Tension dug lines around his eyes, around eyes so dark she could never know what truly lived in his heart. "Haven't you felt that in my touch? Heard it in my voice?"

"Nay, I have not seen one true act of love. Not one. But plenty

165

of caring and kindness and treating the unwanted wife well. I have my pride, Jonah. I am worth being loved. Truly loved. I already know you're not capable of it."

Bitterness rushed across her tongue and she tore away from him, hating that part of her that had always held such foolish dreams. "I'm going to fetch Grandfather. He'll see that you leave."

"Go ahead. Ely will listen to me."

"Nay, he has been unable to keep any hired help, so at least I am useful here. And I know what I'm getting in return."

She turned her back and walked fast and hard away from him, now that her angry words had attracted her grandfather's attention. He would not let Jonah into the house, she was sure of it. She hid in the parlor, took a deep breath, and tried to will the terrible roiling pain out of her heart.

She'd never been special to him. Not she, Tessa Bradford. She would never be the woman he dreamed of at night or in the quiet moments of the day.

He still wanted a convenient, practical marriage. But she did not. She never did. She never would.

She peeked around the corner and he was still there, standing in the rain at the open door. Wind lashed his black hair across his strong chiseled face. Rain soaked his shirt and the white fabric clung to him like a second skin, showing the breadth of his powerful shoulders and every fascinating muscle in his chest and abdomen.

Their gazes locked and he just stared at her. He looked so lost. Her throat tightened, and she knelt to feed the fire in the parlor's hearth, where Violet, her sister, and Charity all lay, consumed with fever.

She turned her back on Jonah and vowed not to cry another tear.

From this day on, she would not want, would not wish. She would not dream foolish dreams again.

CHAPTER FIFTEEN

"You cannot go marching up to her grandfather's house and steal her back." Thomas' fist collided with the table, sending cups and spoons clattering. "She is a woman with feelings, not a stolen piece of furniture."

"I do not intend to steal her. I have thought this over for two days. For two days she does not speak to me. Her grandfather comes at me with a musket. I only intend to take back my wife."

"Mayhap you shouldn't have hurt her so deeply in the first place."

"Aye, I admit it. I was wrong. I was wrong to think—" He steeled his heart, refusing to feel any more of the well-deep pain. But it did not work. "I cannot both hold her and drive the horses. I need help."

"I don't think that is a rational solution."

Considering the sharp and fiery pain raging through his chest, dragging her home seemed like a rational plan. As rational as he could possibly be.

"Ah, true love," Father chuckled from his place at the table, sipping real tea for once. "A fiery thing, that wife of yours. My advice is to surrender. 'Tis the best way to deal with an angry woman. I'd have thought you were smart enough to figure that out, boy. Then again, I never married such a strong-willed woman."

"Tessa will see reason. I know she will. She's my wife and she belongs here with me." In truth, he did not think he could keep going without her. She'd left an emptiness in his life and a worse one in his heart. He did not think he needed to admit such a vulnerability, not even to his family.

"You have much to learn about a woman, boy. Why—"

"Stop it, both of you," Thomas roared. "I can't believe I am hearing this. Tessa is a person with feelings. Her pain should not be trivialized with insincerity, Father. As for you, Jonah, she truly loved you. What do you think will convince her to risk her heart a second time?"

His love. 'Twould have to be enough.

A knock rattled the back door before Jonah could admit the truth aloud. Andy, coughing and pale, was closest to the door and hopped up to open it.

"Major?" The reverend stood in the threshold with the cheery morning sun slanting over him, forcing him to squint. "I apologize for interrupting your morning meal, but Anya sent me."

"Anya?" Jonah pushed out his chair and stood. "Is there a problem? She went to the Bradford's to help Tessa tend her family."

"You have not heard? The Bradford children are all recovering. 'Tis Tessa who is ill."

"Ill?" He crossed the room in two strides. "It cannot be. I saw her just two, nay, three days ago."

The reverend's face saddened, and Jonah heard the knell of grief. " 'Tis true, Jonah. I know you and your wife have had some kind of a disagreement, but now is not the time for conflict. She is gravely ill, mayhap dying. She didn't want you to come, but she has lost consciousness and Anya and I thought it best that you see her."

A cold shock struck him like a blow, left him reeling but unable to feel.

"We'll go together." Thomas' hand settled upon Jonah's shoulder. "Reverend Brown, is there much hope?"

"Nay." Sorrowful. "Tessa is the healer, and now that she is sick, there's no one but Anya to tend her. She cares, but she is not skilled."

"Then we'll call a surgeon. It helped Father." Jonah's mind whirled. He could send Thomas, who would be swiftest, and mayhap—

"There is no time. 'Tis why I'm here. I thought you might want to say goodbye to your wife."

Jonah saw the unavoidable truth in the reverend's eyes, and the compassion. For once, he could not hide, could not seal off his heart, could not freeze out the emotions battering his chest like a horned bull.

His heart cracked wide open. Tears stung his eyes and rolled down his cheeks.

"How long has she been like this?" Jonah demanded as Ely opened the door.

"Two days." The rotund man blocked the threshold. "She left strict instructions. You are not welcome here."

"Move aside, Bradford," Jonah growled, "or I'll tear you limb from limb with my bare hands."

The fleshy man stepped aside.

Jonah caught a dim impression of a filthy kitchen, dishes stacked in piles on the messy board table, the room abandoned. Maybe the others in this house had left for Charity's mother's home, to recover now that Tessa could not tend them. That knowledge sparked another wave of rage. He burst into the parlor and saw the pallet on the floor by the hearth.

Damn Ely. He could not even spare a bed?

"Master Jonah, you came." Anya sprang up from the floor, fatigue bruising her face, harsh around her frightened eyes. "The reverend thought he could convince you to come. Mistress Tessa made me swear not to send for you, but she's unconscious. So, I am not directly breaking my oath to her."

Jonah's throat tightened at the sight of his wife restless with fever beneath a linen sheet. Somehow he managed to speak. "You stayed all day and night with her."

"Aye." Sadness knelled in that quiet word. "I don't know what else to do. I have applied the onion poultice and her lungs are not the problem now. Her fever is. I have used the compresses. I have soaked her in water. She became so chilled I dared not do it more."

Jonah sank to his knees, his gaze never straying from Tessa's face, her dear face. He knew without looking the exact delicate cut of her jaw and chin and cheekbones, the shape of her silken mouth, of her small nose and dark lashes. Every part of her was etched in his memory, engraved in his heart.

He took her hand within his. Her skin felt far too hot, and he saw the blotchy redness marking her skin. The delirium twisted incomprehensible words from her mouth as she thrashed, the fever almost winning its battle.

Too late for a surgeon to bleed her, and he knew nothing about treating illnesses.

" 'Tis up to God now," the reverend said, his boots barely tapping on the floorboards as he stepped into the room. "And up to Tessa."

"You're wrong, Reverend." Jonah pressed his lips to Tessa's knuckles and closed his eyes. " 'Tis up to me, too."

How could he endure losing her? What if he never saw her again? Never to explain he loved her. How he loved her.

"Anya, keep applying compresses. Wasn't there a powder she used on the Hollingsworth child? I know she used it on Father."

"Aye, but I am not certain of the dosage. I can't simply give her any amount, for the powder is dangerous and too much could kill her."

"Well, the fever is already killing her." Jonah shoved past Thomas who had just come from the stable. "Brother, go upstairs and grab the first bed you see and bring it down here. They have Tessa lying on the floor."

"Damn that Ely." A fury matching his own snapped in Thomas' eyes. "I'll find the softest mattress."

Listening to his brother's boots striking angrily on the wood floor, Jonah turned to study Tessa's basket. "This is the bird dropping tea."

" 'Tis not made of bird droppings." Anya grabbed the crock and checked on its contents. 'Twas nearly empty. "But of bark and leaves."

"And this is the other tea that clears congestion."

"Aye, but it does naught for fever."

Jonah pushed aside that crock to reach more. One held bark for headaches, according to Anya, and another dried berries which helped with fever, but not one as severe as Tessa's.

"This is what she used on Mercy Hollingsworth, whose fever was the most severe." Anya hesitantly touched the lid of a small crock. "I wasn't in the kitchen when she crushed the root, and I remember she said 'Tis lethal, even in small quantities, but the right amount can help break a fever."

"Then there is hope?"

"Aye, I've not been sure what to do all night." The young girl's face crumpled with torment. "I cannot sit here and let the woman who gave me a good home die. And yet, how could I live with myself if I gave her the wrong dose?"

"Crush some of the powder. She's too far gone with fever. I have seen it on the battlefield. She is living her nightmares and soon she will be gone to us."

"Aye. I've seen it too." Anya bowed her head. "You will administer the powder? I'm no coward, and yet, I cannot hurt my mistress. I could never—"

Jonah's throat ached. "I will administer the powder."

Tears rolled down Anya's face as she dropped a small black root into a shallow bowl.

He helped his brother bring down a bed, Ely and Charity's, judging by the look of it. And in no time assembled it in front of the fire, laid the sheets and eased Tessa's fitful body upon it.

She was fighting the fever, this he knew. He sat on the edge of the feather mattress, taking both of her hands in his. Her head thrashed from side to side, and her ebony curls were plastered with sweat. Her legs kicked and her body twisted. She suffered, and he hated it.

He released her hands with a kiss to her knuckles and wrung die cool herbed water from a cloth soaking in a nearby pail. He folded it into thirds and laid the compress on her forehead, another on her throat, and so on, until her body was swathed in white and he started the process over again.

Thomas ran to the well for more cold water, and Anya mixed the herbs for them. They ran out of cloths, and the reverend raced next door to borrow what he could from the Sandersons.

A knock rattled the door. Jonah soaked more cloths in the fresh water while Thomas answered it. Susan Hollingsworth stood in the threshold with a basket on her arm.

"I brought food and more clean linens." The woman seemed hesitant. "I don't want to interrupt, but I heard Tessa was ill. She saved my girls' lives many times over the years and now is the first chance I've had to pay back some of her kindness."

" 'Tis appreciated," Jonah managed.

"I will put on some of my soup to warm." Susan set the basket down on a low table and rifled through it. "This is for Tessa. My girls made it for her. As a thank you."

Jonah took the small rag doll, made with inexperienced stitches, but all the more dear with thanks. He sat it on the headboard above Tessa. The doll with uneven black yarn hair smiled crookedly down at her.

"Jo-nah," she whispered brokenly in her sleep.

She was not awake; she didn't know he was at her side. He lifted the cloth from her brow and replaced it with a fresh one.

"Jo-nah, Jonah, nooooo." So heartbroken that sound, so lost and desolate.

He laid a hand to her cheek, and his heart hurt like sunshine cracking hard layers of ice, like spring come to the land.

"I have the blackbale powder." Anya gazed down at the bed, at Tessa who stared up at them in delirium, not seeing them, not seeing anything. "Susan, do you remember how much of this Tessa gave to Mercy?"

"Nay, I was too distraught to notice, I'm ashamed to say." Susan knelt at the bedside, her hands clenched.

Thomas stood behind her, his face shadowed. The reverend crowded close, opening his well-worn Bible.

Jonah pressed a kiss to his wife's cheek and dropped a pinch of the ground powder on the center of her tongue.

Now, they waited. He set the little bowl aside and took Tessa's hands, determined to hold her, to stand beside her until the very end.

CHAPTER SIXTEEN

Tessa opened her eyes. Sunshine, warm and merry, slashed through the generous window of the room. She recognized the diamond paned windows and the chest of drawers and her mother's trunk leaned against the wall.

"So, you're finally awake."

She recognized that voice too, rum rich and rumbling like tempered thunder. She turned her head on the pillow and saw him seated in a chair at her side. Dark circles rimmed his eyes, and lines crinkled around the bold cut of his mouth. He looked like a man who hadn't slept in many nights.

"Why am I here? I don't live here anymore. I don't understand." Her chest felt tight and her whole body felt achy. "I want to go home."

"You are home, now and forever." Warm strong fingers encircled hers, holding her in a grip that felt possessive and claiming, the way a man holds a wife he loves. "I brought you here as soon as the fever broke. I couldn't stand seeing you in Bradford's house, not when you have a place where you're loved and cherished."

"Jonah, nay, I—"

" 'Tis the truth. I love you." A slow curve of his mouth drew her gaze, but it was the true emotion in his eyes that surprised her, emotion bright as a thousand suns and twice as everlasting.

Hope grew within, sweet and new.

"I cannot live without you. I know that now." His kiss brushed her knuckles. "I will never be anything without you. Because you married me, and opened wide my heart."

"But you never loved me. You never loved—" Tears burned, and she turned her head away. She was not strong enough for this. She was thirsty and nauseous and tremblingly weak from the fever. Even the sun hurt her eyes.

"You are wrong, Tessa. I loved you all along. Why else would I have given my life over to you? And maybe, just maybe, I thought of that ridiculous way to choose a wife because deep down inside I knew it was you who would offer. You were the one I wanted."

"Jonah." How could this be true? And yet throughout their marriage he *had* cared for her. He'd made sure she had rest and meals. He'd found a servant so she would not have to work hard, and bought her clothes, and even took her to the seamstress.

And most of all, he'd taken care of her when she was ill. He'd stayed by her side, just as he'd done for his father.

No one had ever cared for her that much.

"I had the same dream over and over when I was sick." She dared to look at him, the love she felt for him growing stronger once again.

"You called my name when you were feverish." He shifted on the chair, drawing closer so that she could see his capable shoulders and rock-hard chest and the handsome way his slow smile changed his face.

"Aye. I dreamed we were in the forest together and you told me you no longer wanted me. 'Twas horrible, and you left me, running away into the mists, and I couldn't find you."

"An impossible nightmare. How could I leave you?" He pressed a tender kiss to her cheek. "You have my heart. Every last bit of it. For now and forever."

She gazed up at him and saw what she'd never seen before. He understood that the quiet challenge of loving another took the greatest courage. But he was a courageous man—her own hero—and she knew with unending certainty he would love her every moment of every day.

"Come, I want to show you something." He pulled back the covers.

"I'm not strong enough to walk."

"Then I will carry you."

He gathered her into his arms, and how wondrous it felt to be cradled against his chest.

"I had much time to think whilst we waited for your fever to break." He navigated the stairs with ease, holding her close.

"What? *You* were thinking?"

"Aye, 'Tis shocking, I know. But every once in awhile I am capable of it. And I did see what a thick-skulled dolt I was. I should warn you that I'll probably show this trait from time to time, for it runs in my family. Surely you've noticed this same fault in my brothers."

"Now, I heard that." Thomas looked up from his Sunday afternoon reading.

Andy closed his book. " 'Tis good to see you awake, sister. Mayhap I should fetch you some tea."

"That sounds wonderful," she answered as Jonah lowered her onto a hard wooden bench. She didn't remember a bench being in their comfortable parlor. In fact, much had changed since she last saw this room.

Andy scampered off, footsteps echoing in the nearly empty room, on the floors without carpets, on walls without tapestries, on windows without curtains.

"What is this?"

A wicked grin teased dimples into his cheeks and a mischievous spark twinkled in eyes as dark as midnight. "All our furniture is in Mistress Briers' stable. She has agreed to upholster it anew for you."

"For me?"

"Aye, you are the lady of this house now, Tessa. 'Tis your home, and you should make it yours." His fingertips brushed curls out of her eyes, an infinitely tender act. "Besides, you know the place. What do four men know about decorating? 'Twas an eyesore. We're depending on you to save us from our lack of taste."

"Not again?"

"Aye. I need your skills yet again." Humor twinkled in eyes as dark as a devil's.

And she saw it then, as the colonel ambled into the room with a book in hand and Thomas sat awaiting her answer with hope in his eyes and Andy returned holding a cup of steaming tea just for her.

This was her family, her real family, and they loved her as she loved them.

Her husband, her wonderful husband, stood and took the cup from his brother. "So, what do you think?"

"This needing me is becoming a habit. First I save your father and brother. Then I find Anya to save your sorry souls. And now you want new furnishings."

"Aye. I might very well need you for the rest of my life." He knelt before her, but it was love that blended with the glinting humor in his eyes, love that gentled his voice. "Especially since I will be needing a son or daughter."

And how wickedly he said it, as if he wanted to haul her back upstairs and lay her down in that bed—Even weak, she felt desire pool hot and low.

"All right, Jonah. As you know, I'm always a dutiful wife."

That made him laugh. She could see it now. There would be children racing around these rooms, the colonel watching them over the top of his book, and Jonah at her side.

"Andy, what kind of tea did you bring me?" She sniffed at the bitter brew.

"Why, 'Tis your bird dropping tea, of course." Andy grinned, and she recognized the slant of revenge in that unabashed grin.

The colonel threw back his head and laughed. "That a boy, give her a dose of her own medicine. Then she'll know how we have suffered."

"Drink it, sweet Tessa." Jonah kissed her brow again. "For I want my beloved wife well and strong. We have such a wondrous life ahead of us."

Garnet's Treasure

Montana Territory—1864

Night deepened as Garnet Jones climbed off the stagecoach and studied what she could see of the dark mining town. There wasn't much. Small campfires glowed like embers on a flat expanse of ground. On the other side of the street the many windows of saloons and brothels lit up the darkness.

Garnet heard a gunshot explode inside one of the buildings. A woman screamed. A man shouted.

"I'm scared," fifteen-year-old Golda whispered, clinging to the side of the stagecoach. "Maybe we shouldn't have come."

"We had no choice." Garnet thought of Pa and the letter she'd received. The man had fathered her and she had a duty to him, no matter how tempting turning back may be.

"Welcome to Stinking Creek, ma'am," the stagecoach driver announced. He threw down their few bags. The valises hit the ground with a muffled thunk, kicking up thick plumes of dust. "This here's the end of the line."

Well, they were in the right town, but it wasn't an impressive place. Or a particularly nice-smelling one. Garnet wrinkled her nose, staring briefly at a dirty, obviously drunk miner doing his personal business on the walkway between the brothel and the saloon. "Don't look, Golda."

Golda snapped her head so fast, she nearly lost her balance in order to stare in amazement and perhaps curiosity at the indecent sight.

"I said, don't look," Garnet instructed, her indignation growing with each shaky breath. The golden glow from the well-lit tavern glinted through the large window, illuminating him clearly. He had the audacity to tip his hat to her, his business now done, before striding back into the saloon to liquor himself up further.

"I know why they call it Stinking Creek." Garnet shook her head. This was just the sort of place she should have expected. Some derelict mining camp without a bit of civilization.

Perhaps Golda was right. Perhaps they shouldn't have come. Perhaps they should have sent a communication from Virginia City instead.

"Struck gold here last summer. Not a good strike, mind ya. And it ain't the safest camp around." The stooped, foul-smelling driver stepped closer and picked up their few bags. He wheezed when he spoke. "A man was murdered a while back. Are you sure you wanna stay, ma'am? Only the workin' kinda girls come to this town. I don't think we've had no quality ladies like yerselves here before. Unless you two, uh, are looking to, uh, find employment."

"We're staying, and not to find work." Garnet clucked her tongue as she gave the little man a hard look. Certainly he wasn't suggesting she was a soiled dove. Appalled by the mere thought of it, she snatched Golda's bags from his despicable grip and shoved them into her younger sister's arms.

"I ken take you girls back to Virginia City. This ain't no place for the likes of you." The driver spat a stream of foul brown juice into the dirt at his feet. He bent stiffly to lift up her valise, but Garnet was quicker.

She snatched the sturdy handles firmly before he could toss her belongings back aboard. She was staying, whether she liked it or not. "This is hardly my idea of paradise, but that can't be helped. I must find our pa. He's staying with a Mr. Tanner. Do you know him?"

The driver stood, thinking deeply. Using his brain was clearly an effort. The glow from the tavern's window brushed the driver's face with orange and black shadows while he ruminated. "Tanner? He lives just out that-a-way." He pointed an age-crooked finger away from town, where the dark shades and shadows of night beckoned.

"Do you know how far?"

"Not too far. Keeps to himself, though. Ain't the social type." The driver spat again. "I don't reckon a nice gal like you wants to see Wyatt Tanner."

"Why not?" Garnet felt a chill prickle at the nape of her neck.

"Folks say he's dangerous."

"Dangerous?"

"Deadly." The driver shivered as if he were afraid, too. "Well, I gotta get going, missy. You gals take care of yerselves."

Golda gasped, and her fingers gripped Garnet's arm with a panicked clench. "Did you hear what he said? A man was murdered. We're not safe here. Oh, we never should have come."

"You're the one who didn't want to leave Pa here by himself. And since we're here, we'd best not panic," Garnet replied, sensibly. "You know we can't up and abandon Pa now, not after we've traveled so far."

"I guess not." Golda sighed heavily. "But I'm still frightened."

Truth be told, so was Garnet.

The stagecoach rolled away, spewing up black clouds of dust into the air like fog. Garnet coughed, quickly covering her face with a handkerchief. The dust stuck in her throat so she could hardly breathe. But that wasn't the worst of her problems. Not by a long shot. They were alone in the middle of the night in a disreputable mining camp looking for a dangerous man. Another term of school teaching was a more inviting prospect than this.

"What do we do now?" Golda's voice wobbled.

"We find a hotel room for the night."

"Do you think they have a nice hotel in a place like this?" Golda choked on a little sob.

Garnet gazed about the sorry excuse for a town. The moonless sky left the faces of the buildings in shadows as she stood, eyes adjusting to the darkness. Fear shivered down her spine, but she shrugged it away. She hadn't traveled all this way to be frightened. She had a job to do, and, by golly, nothing would stop her.

"Come." She took hold of Golda's gloved hand. "Maybe there's a better place down the block."

"But it's so dark."

It was dark, but the buildings lining the streets were lighted and, from the look of it, filled to capacity. She could hear the shouts of men in the saloons, the jeering argument over a card game, and the tinny piano music filtering out into the street like lamplight.

This was not a decent town.

Perhaps she had best rethink her plan. She had not expected the West to be quite so . . . rough.

"I see you're just off the stage," a woman's friendly voice called out. "You girls looking for work?"

"What kind of work?" Oh. Garnet remembered the stage driver's words. "No, I guess we aren't working girls."

"Too bad. We could use more help. It's real busy this time of year."

Garnet stared at the woman, who posed in a lighted doorway of what could only be a brothel. Goodness, she'd never held a conversation with a prostitute before. Then again, ever since she'd left Willow Hollow, nothing had been the same.

"Are you girls lost?" the soiled dove asked, ever helpful. "Speak up, so's I can help you out. This ain't no town where a body should be standing around on the street."

Before Garnet could answer, a gunshot exploded from somewhere inside one of the saloons. A horrible, hairsplitting whiz buzzed past Garnet's head and a bullet lodged into the wooden wall of a trough not two feet away. Water spilled through the bullet hole, running out onto the dry, dusty earth.

Garnet stared at the stream of water winking in the small bit of light from the open brothel door. Her knees knocked. She didn't like this town. Not one little bit. "We're, ah, looking for a hotel."

"A hotel? There ain't anything like that here." The woman chuckled. "Did you girls take the wrong stage?"

"I wish we had." Garnet glanced up and down the street, wondering when the next bullet might split the air. Or knock them both to the ground dead. "Maybe you could help us. I'm looking for Mr. Wyatt Tanner. He has been kind enough to look after my ill father, and I've come to retrieve him."

"Ah." The soiled dove nodded. "Wyatt is a . . ."

"A dangerous man?" Garnet supplied.

"Yes." The woman shrugged, a simple gesture. "Wyatt doesn't like people. It might be best if you girls waited until morning to hunt him down. Perhaps we could find you a room for the night. Maybe something . . ." she hesitated.

"Respectable?" Garnet offered.

"I'll try."

"I'd rather just find Pa," Golda said quietly. Her voice quaked in fear. "I worry he's dead by now. That we've arrived too late."

Garnet closed her eyes. She was tired, afraid, and did not want to stand out on this street any longer. She feared more than bullets. Who knew what type of men frequented that saloon, gambled and . . . *recreated* in those buildings? If she breathed deeply she could smell the horrible condition of the town—the result of too many men living on their own without a woman's firm guidance and good judgment. Dear Lord, didn't men have enough sense in their big heads to know how to sweep and wash and bathe?

"Well, if you would rather, Wyatt's cabin is the last at the end of town." The woman said Mr. Tanner's given name as if she knew him well. As if she . . . Garnet didn't complete that thought.

"The last cabin, you say?"

"Yes. Just walk that-a-way toward the mountains, and you can't miss it."

"Thank you," Garnet said cordially and turned. Hitching her skirts high, she carefully stepped over several tobacco juice stains left by the stagecoach driver and the round, telltale wet patch beside the saloon.

"Suppose it isn't safe to be walking down these streets," Golda whispered, standing frozen with fear in the dusty road. "Especially in the dark."

Several gunshots rang out inside one of the buildings, and Garnet winced. No bullets buzzed past her, but she didn't feel safe. Through an uncovered window, she could see the inside of one of the many saloons. A woman dressed in red with her bosom showing danced on the top of a table. The men's hoots and jeers resounded in the cool night air.

This was simply not a surprise. Leave it to their pa, weak in morals, to end up in a despicable camp such as this. She doubted if there was even a church in town. Well, there was simply no alternative. They could not stand about on the street all night waiting for the next whizzing bullet. Garnet grabbed her sister by the arm and tugged. They started down the street.

"What if we can't find Pa after all?" Golda whispered. "What if he's already gone? What if we've come all this way for nothing?"

"Pa had better still be alive," Garnet bit out harshly enough so she didn't sound quite so afraid. "The hardship that man has placed upon this family is a disgrace. If he isn't dead, then he had better start praying. When I catch up to him, I'll—"

"Garnet," Golda hissed. "Look. Someone's coming toward us."

A shadow moved up ahead on the darker part of the street where no buildings stood. There was little light to make out what moved there, but from the sound of the footfalls, Garnet didn't need to wonder. She knew. Another irresponsible man who would rather cause trouble, break the law, or play with his guns and his patch of dirt than hold a respectable job. The town was probably packed with vile men just like him.

"Howdy girls," he called out, rough and deep, and he changed his direction just to intercept them. "Are ya havin' a slow night?"

Garnet stared at the man, deeply repulsed at his friendliness. Goodness, they were decent women. He was dressed so darkly she could hardly make him out except for the flash of guns strapped to both thighs. The sight made her heart quake.

He strolled closer, his chuckle deep as he called out, "How much'll it cost me fer both of ya?"

Golda whimpered, and Garnet skidded to a halt. Cost him? For what? Indignation rolled over her, stealing away some of her fear. He thought they were selling their charms on the street. Why, she'd simply never been mistaken for a . . . heavens, she had never been so insulted.

"I said, how much?"

"How much?" Garnet hissed. "A decent woman is worth more than you can pay."

"Is that so?" The man cocked one eyebrow, interested now. "I got me a lot of gold."

"A lot of gold?" Oh, she was mad. "Is that all?"

"Ain't that enough?"

Garnet thought of how Pa had left them over the years. "A woman wants much more than a bit of silly dust. She requires substance of character and steadfast integrity. Both of which you obviously lack."

She glared at the sorry excuse for a man. It was evident he had no moral fiber. He'd probably abandoned a wife and half a dozen children just to hunt for gold in the wilderness.

Just like her pa had.

Deplorable. Simply deplorable. She had no notion what the

world was coming to.

The man blushed furiously and ran off in the night.

A lot of gold indeed! Garnet huffed. No wonder Pa had found his way here. He was among his kind—shiftless men who dreamed of achieving fortunes without an honest day's labor. She was greatly displeased to see for herself the depth to which civilization would sink without a woman's firm hand. Surely they could locate Pa, board him on the next stage out of town, and be away from this foul camp.

If she could survive the smell.

COMING SOON!

ABOUT THE AUTHOR

Jillian Hart makes her home in Washington State, where she has lived most of her life. When Jillian is not writing away on her next book, she can be found reading, going to lunch with friends and spending quiet evenings at home with her family.

Made in the USA
San Bernardino, CA
04 September 2013